The Pauper

His Searchers

Book 5

By

Ronna M. Bacon

Isaiah 40:29-31

29 He gives power to the weak, And to those who have no might He increases strength.

30 Even the youths shall faint and be weary, and the young men shall utterly fall,

31 But those who wait on the Lord shall renew their strength; they shall mount up with wings like eagles, they shall run and not be weary, they shall walk and not faint.

Jeremiah 1714

14 Heal me, LORD, and I will be healed; save me and I will be saved, for you are the one I praise.

NKJV

Table of Contents

Chapter 1
Chapter 2
Chapter 3
Chapter 4
Chapter 5
Chapter 6
Chapter 7
Chapter 8
Chapter 9
Chapter 10
Chapter 11
Chapter 12
Chapter 13
Chapter 14
Chapter 15
Chapter 16
Chapter 17
Chapter 18
Chapter 19
Chapter 20
Chapter 21
Chapter 22
Chapter 23
Chapter 24
Chapter 25
Chapter 26
Chapter 27
Chapter 28
Chapter 29
Chapter 30

Chapter 31
Chapter 32
Chapter 33
Chapter 34
Chapter 35
Chapter 36
Chapter 37
Chapter 38
Chapter 39
Chapter 40
Chapter 41
Chapter 42
Chapter 43
Chapter 44
Chapter 45
Chapter 46
Epilogue
Dear Readers

Chapter 1

The fresh air of a mid-fall predawn morning greeted Avery Dennis as he shoved open the door of his SUV and then just sat, one foot resting on the pavement of the parking lot. He stared at the building he was headed for, a place he loved to be, but today? He just didn't want to be there. Avery's right wrist rested on the steering wheel, his deep brown eyes thoughtful. He knew why he was restless. Seeing his brother and sister both settled with their life mates? That stirred a wish within him, that he had someone of his very own, someone to share the solitary life that he had been living and change it. *God, where are You? Is there someone there for me? Or am I destined to live life on my own?* He ran his free hand through his dark auburn hair, worry tugging at him for a moment.

He reached for the travel mug of coffee in the console and then for the small paper bag with his breakfast sandwich. *Sitting here isn't getting to work, am I,* he thought? Now what? *Do I go in or do I play hooky? Unfortunately, I have to.* Avery swung the door closed, his sigh once more rising within him. He trudged towards the back door that he usually entered, stepping through it and pausing. Avery frowned, feeling something was off but not sure what that was or why he was feeling like that. It had been fine when he walked away three days ago. It must just be because it's Monday, Avery thought, heading for the office where he set down his mug and sandwich, shrugging

—

7

out of his jean jacket and draping that across the back of his chair.

His head tilting, Avery listened to the sounds of the music that came from the studio, knowing that he would be in there shortly. He worked the early morning shift, playing the golden oldies as they were called, music from decades ago. His friends asked how he could even listen to that music, but he always grinned. It was the music that he enjoyed and had no problems playing it. Avery also shrugged when he was told that a Christian shouldn't listen to that music and simply asked that person, why not? Did God say that they couldn't or shouldn't? That person had not had a response, simply glaring at him before walking away in a huff.

The sounds of another person moving around drew his attention and he frowned for a moment, before he was in the hallway, searching. He was usually on his own and to have someone else here? Avery paused at the door to the reception area, a frown once more on his face. He didn't know the lady who sat at the desk, only knowing that a new receptionist would be starting. He just didn't expect to see her there that earlier.

Kitlin MacTavish paused in her movements, sensing someone near her. She sighed, knowing that she had to look up and just not wanting to. She had been hired as the new receptionist at the radio station, given the keys and told to report early in the morning every day. She didn't like that. Kitlin felt something off about it but just couldn't put her finger on it. Moving to Riverville had taken just about all the courage that she could muster up. She didn't do well in new places or with new people, but God had prompted her to pack her things and move there. Just why that was? Kitlin had no idea.

Her deep blue eyes rose, searching for the man who had been dogging her footsteps. She didn't know him or know why he was chasing her, but he was. Friends had been asked about her but had refused to say anything, other than to warn her. Her golden blond curls moved as her head did, and then she froze. A man stood in the shadowy doorway and that scared her. No, terrified her, she decided.

"Hi!" Avery moved forward, into the dim lighting of the reception area. "I'm sorry. I didn't know someone else was here. I'm usually on my own this early. I'm Avery Dennis." His baritone voice held a question for her, but also soothed her fears.

"Hi. I'm Kitlin MacTavish. I'm the new receptionist. Or at least, I think I am." Kitlin rose, tugging her aqua-coloured sweater down over her jeans. She paced the area, moving towards the window and peeking through the drapes and then back to the door, checking the locks. She stared around, taking in the comfortable leather chairs, a table with pamphlets and magazines on it, the potted plants, and the framed photos on the walls showing the station's history over time.

Avery perched on the corner of the desk, his arms folded across his chest, puzzled at her movements.

—

"Kitlin? What's wrong? You're pacing and somehow I don't think that's you."

Kitlin spun, startled, having forgotten for a moment that Avery was there. Her eyes were huge as she stared at him.

"I forgot that you were here." She frowned at him. "And just why are you here this early?"

"I host the morning golden oldies show. Didn't they give you a list of who does what?" He was puzzled even more at her response.

Kitlin sank into one of the chairs, her face dropping into her hands. He had found her, she decided. Whoever it was? He had found her. She could feel him outside.

"He's here, isn't he?" Her words were barely audible.

"Who is?" Avery rose, coming to drop into a crouch beside her, a hand reaching to rest on her shoulder. "Who are you afraid of, Kitlin? And can I help?"

Shaking her head, Kitlin knew that she had to explain what she meant. Only she had no way of knowing if Avery would help or not. He was a stranger to her.

"Kitlin? Let me help you. You're new to town and we don't like it when our new friends are scared. The police chief is my cousin and I have many friends on the force. We'll protect you." Avery was becoming very worried about her. He heard a soft sound at the back door and looked that way for a moment. His attention then went back to Kitlin.

"I'm sorry. Your cousin?" Kitlin's hands dropped and she stared at him, not quite sure to believe him.

"Caleb? He's the police chief. And I do have people that you can talk to. Let me help you."

Kitlin kept staring at him, her eyes huge as she did so. This is not what she had expected to hear. He was a stranger to her but he was offering to help. She raised her eyes to the doorway and a scream was torn from her. Avery began to spin and rise, freezing as he did so, his hands raising in the air.

The masked men stood for a moment before the weapons were pointed at them. Avery rose to his feet, a hand reaching for Kitlin's. She grasped at his fingers, fear causing her to shake. She had been found but now what? She stared at the men, not sure what was happening. Avery's fingers tightened on hers, even as he was moved backwards and towards the front door.

One of the men shoved it open, peeking out and then beckoning for them to follow. They were shoved from the building, across the parking lot, and then into a waiting cube van. Forced to the floor, their hands were bound and gags wrapped around their mouths. Kitlin moved as close to Avery as she could, seeking protection and comfort as they felt the van picking up speed.

Avery grew angry, angry that he was helpless to get Kitlin to safety, angry that they had been taken, but also puzzled and worried as to just why. He didn't have any enemies, at least not that he was aware of. He began to pray, begging God to free them and to protect them.

Kitlin was terrified, she had to admit. She had no idea why this had happened. Was it her or Avery? She just couldn't think, fear had taken that ability away from her. She leaned against Avery, seeking to draw from his strength. Only, she didn't know him to know that he would do everything within his power to protect her, well that and God's strength. Avery had no doubt that God was in control and that He had allowed this. Only neither one of them knew exactly why.

Chapter 2

Rubbing a hand along the back of his neck, Tommy Streetlander, turned in a circle in the reception area of the radio station. Streeter as he was commonly known as, his call name from his on-air days, was puzzled. There was no sign of either Avery or Kitlin, and there should be. It was Monday, and Avery always had the early morning show. Kitlin? As the receptionist, her hours started at 7 as the phones began to ring once live music started. The station had pre-arranged programming that ran overnight. Streeter paced back through the building, stopping in the office doorway and nodding. Yes, he thought, Avery had been there. His travel mug and sandwich that he always brought with him were on the desk, his jacket on the chair back.

Caleb Logan, Riverville police chief, stood watching him, a frown on his face. No, he thought, something is off. Avery would not just abandon his time on the air. Even if something had happened, he would have called for help. Sudden fear hit him. Was another of his wife, Hannah's, cousins to face danger? That became his fear.

"Streeter?" Caleb moved to stand beside Streeter, watching as a patrol officer entered from the back door, stopping to study the lock. "Where are they?"

"Caleb? I have no idea. It's not Avery to walk away and not show up. He calls if he can't make it and arranges for someone to cover for him. Kitlin? She was so thankful to get work that she was eager to be here." Streeter paused as he saw the officer turning away from the door and then studying the floor. He sighed. "We have to leave?"

"It would be best. I want to bring in a detective and a crime scene unit." Caleb pointed back towards the front door. "That way, please."

Streeter nodded, worry evident on his face. His employees were like family to him, he thought. There was no friction between them, not that he was aware of.

"Okay, Streeter. Talk to me." Caleb watched as Frankie Brennan, head detective on the force, headed his way. "Here's Frankie. He'll need to know what you can tell us."

Frankie nodded, a pen and his notepad appearing in his hands.

"Streeter? What can you tell us?"

Streeter stared around, seeing Avery's vehicle parked in its normal spot. And there was Kitlin's bicycle, chained to the bike rack. He had questioned her about riding a bicycle but she was adamant that she did when the weather was good. It was her, she simply stated.

"I don't know much. Megan called me just after seven. Becky and I were on the back deck, enjoying our morning coffee like we always do. She asked if Avery was not in today. That were was only static on the air. He always takes over the airwaves at seven in the morning on weekdays. I turned on the radio and found that she was correct. I rushed down here, found the building open as it is in the morning, but no sign of the two of them. Avery's travel mug and the breakfast sandwich he picks up are on his desk, his jacket on the chair. Kitlin's sweatshirt is on her chair. There is just no sign of them."

Frankie turned to study the building, worry that he wouldn't show growing within him. Another friend, he thought, to face danger. Only there are no signs of anything. No signs of where they went. And that was not Avery. He would not do that to them, not after what Aveleen and Aubrey had gone through. Aveleen had disappeared twice on them, for months at a time, and Aubrey had been through too much as well. *Lord, where are they? Where are our friends? I know that You are in control but we need to find them and find them fast.*

"Avery was due in this morning, right?" Frankie watched as Streeter nodded. "Then, he was here and disappeared? Your security feed?"

"I already called the company. It went off line just around 6:30 this morning and hasn't gone back on." Streeter was puzzled at that. "We have it set up to go wireless if the power goes out."

"Only the power didn't go out." Frankie excused himself, walking towards the building, a tech waiting for him.

"Jonesy? What do you have for me?"

"Not what you want to hear. The door was jimmied open. The security system was signed into,

---

but it's not working." Jonesy headed for the security panel. "I can see where someone tried to sign in and thought that they had."

"Streeter said that he checked with the security company. The feed went off line around the time that Avery would have arrived. And it should have gone to a wireless, wifi feed." Frankie stopped in his tracks, his eyes on Jonesy. "That means someone is involved."

"From the security company?" Jonesy nodded. "There are rumours about that company, Frankie, particularly in the last few weeks. Their reputation is going downhill and they are losing business. The business that they're losing? Those companies are concerning. They are in the media line as well as some insurance companies. I've been watching them and have a list I can provide you. A friend works for one of the media companies and talked to me. I think you'll need to look into that."

"Thanks, Jonesy. Get the list to me today if you can. We need to work on finding these two." Frankie stood in the office, staring at Avery's mug. "He was here. The new receptionist was here. Now, they're not. And we don't know who or why. Anything at all that you found?"

Jonesy shook his head.

"They were pros, Frankie. No fingerprints. No evidence at all. Just vanished. And I know Avery would not do that to his family. Not given what they have all been through." Jonesy gave a sad smile. "I talked to Aubrey a week or so ago. He was praying that Avery escaped this. Now, who talks to them?"

Caleb had approached, stopping in the doorway, listening to the conversation, knowing that Frankie would have come to him with what he had been told.

"Frankie? You're the lead investigator. It will be up to you. I just need to break it to Hannah." A yawn caught him off guard.

Frankie had turned, studying his friend and superior. *Caleb, you're tired. What have you done to yourself?*

"Caleb? Are you okay?"

Caleb nodded, rubbing at his eyes.

"I am. Hannah and I were up and down all night. All three kids were up sick over night. Her parents are away and can't help. Peg said she and Marg would head over to help." He mentioned the wives of two retired officers. He looked at Frankie, seeing his sudden grin and nod. "Talk to Eddie and Ben. They may be of help. Ben has so many contacts here in town and so does Eddie."

"I'll plan on that. And also Abe. At some point, we'll need his team." Abe was a good friend but also had a security team that was pulled in to provide protection for their friends. He never said no.

"All right. I'm heading in. Come find me when you have a bit better picture of what we're facing." Caleb walked away, his steps slow for him, leaving Frankie and Jonesy sharing a glance.

—

Chapter 3

Frankie dropped his folders on his desk, draping his jacket over one of the chairs in front of it. He rubbed at his face and then squinted at his watch. It wasn't noon yet and he felt worn out and beat down. There were so many cases to work, and this with Avery? It just added to the burden he was carrying. He stared around his office, not seeing the bookshelves that his wife, Deirdre, had decorated for him, the certificates and awards on the walls, or the couch that he sometimes used when he worked late.

Sighing, Frankie reached for the mug he preferred and headed for the break room. He needed coffee and that he needed badly. He started a new pot and then stood, his head down, his heart praying for his friends. *Where are you, Avery? How did you disappear? And why you? I don't get it, Lord, not at all. He's in a safe job, isn't he?*

Caleb watched for a moment before he approached, a hand resting on Frankie's shoulder before he poured their coffee and tea. He knew that Frankie had just returned to the office, caught up as he was in more than one investigation.

"Frankie? What can you tell me?"

Frankie shook his head, his hand grasping his mug.

"Not a lot, Caleb. There was no evidence of anyone else there, other than the security feed off line.

—

That we can't figure out. It looks as if it's working in the building, but nothing is getting through. It went off just about the time Avery arrived."

"This was planned, then. What do we know about Kitlin MacTavish?"

"Not a lot as yet. We're working on that, but she just moved here from Hope. I reached out to that town's force but the officer I spoke with said he'd have a detective call me. I found that a bit odd."

"It is. Is she on the run or involved in something deep?" Caleb sat on one of the chairs in Frankie's office, his mug hitting the desk.

"That I don't know. I didn't get the sense that she was on the run, other than she wanted to move towns. I did learn that her parents are serving overseas for the government and her brother runs a lawn care company. They're twins." Frankie sighed as his desk phone rang. "I can't catch a break today, Caleb." His finger up to keep Caleb with him, he answered his phone. "Brennan."

"Hello? Is this Detective Brennan?" A voice echoed over the phone.

Frankie frowned.

"This is. Who am I speaking with?"

"My name is Kieren MacTavish. I'm looking for my sister. Her employer asked that I speak with you."

"Kieren MacTavish? Your sister is Kitlin?"

"She is. My twin in fact. Do you know where she is? I had a sudden fear for her this morning."

"No, I don't know where she is. Are you in Hope?"

"No, actually. I'm in Riverville. Sitting outside the police detachment at the moment. What happened to her?"

"Come into the building. I will meet you at the front desk." Frankie was on his feet, shaking his head. "Kitlin's brother is here. Would you stay, Caleb?"

"I will. Go find him. Maybe we can get some answers."

"It would be nice but I wouldn't hold my breath." Frankie disappeared to reappear with a younger man, whose colouring matched his sister's. "Kieren, this is our police chief, Caleb Logan. He would like to be in our talk, if he can."

Kieren shrugged, before he reached to shake Caleb's hand.

"That's okay." He turned in his seat, to face Frankie, worry evident on his face. "What can you tell me? I talked to Kitlin last night. She was excited to start working here, wanting a change. I was to meet her for lunch, but she didn't respond to my text messages. When I went to where she was working, her employer started to say something and then just said that I had to speak with you. Where is she? This is not her."

Frankie studied the younger man, not quite sure how to read him. He shared a look with Caleb who nodded.

"I spoke with an officer in Hope. I understand that your parents are overseas?"

"They are. Dad's about ready to retire and is due home next week. They discussed Kitlin's move with her and agreed that it was the best move for her." Kieren thought back to their discussion, sometimes fiery on Kitlin's part. "She wanted to move away from our home town. Just because, she said. There was no particular reason, other than she wanted to live somewhere else, to be on her own, just to see if she could stand on her own two feet, she said. We're close and we did have words over this. But I love my sister. I didn't want her hurt. But where is she?"

"At the moment, Kitlin is missing."

"Missing?" Kieren's voice rose in shock and then stopped abruptly. "How?"

"Early this morning. We know that she reported to work. Her backpack with her ID, her bike, and her sweatshirt are there. The thing of it? There is someone else missing. The radio host for the early morning show, Avery Dennis, is gone as well."

"Avery Dennis? I listen to his show. He's missing? Who were they after? My sister or him?"

"Why would you ask that?" Caleb spoke at last, his eyes assessing the young man.

Kieren shrugged, not quite sure how to respond.

"Kitlin felt followed here in town, but she thought it was just because she was new here. That someone had seen her and was just trying to make sure that she was safe." Kieren blinked, his emotions taking over for a moment. "But what if that was wrong? What if they meant her harm?"

Chapter 4

Frankie was troubled at what Kieren had just admitted. He shared a look with Caleb, who simply nodded.

"Okay, Kieren. Did she describe anyone at all?"

"No, she didn't, Detective. She couldn't get a real good glimpse of whoever it was. I mean, she loves this town. Even though she has only been here for a few weeks, she feels it is home. She has been welcomed here." Kieren blinked for a moment, his emotions almost overtaking him. "What can you tell me about today?"

Frankie sat back, his eyes on what notes he had taken. There was not a lot that he could share.

"I'm sorry, Kieren. There is not a lot that we know at present. We're just in the early stages of the investigation. I would like to speak with you at length about your sister. Can we meet later this afternoon? I would like to see her apartment, if you have access to it and can agree to that."

Kieren stared at him and then nodded.

"I do. I'm staying there for now. My work is over for the year and I usually take a vacation at this point." He sighed, a deep from the toes sigh. "This year, that's not happening. I just want my sister home and safe. Can you guarantee that?" He was on his feet

---

and walking away, leaving Caleb and Frankie standing watching him.

"He's right, Frankie. We need to find her and bring her home, safe. As well as Avery. You'll be speaking with Aubrey and Aveleen next as well as Michael and Meg."

"That I will. This hurts, you know. That family doesn't need a third member going through anything. And I just don't see the connection between the two, other than the radio station."

"I know. That is the connection, the only one we have at the moment. Have someone start an investigation into that. You have enough with the two disappearing. I can't see Streeter involved in anything illegal."

"No, I can't see that, but we've seen that before. I'll call in Emma as well. She's already calling me."

"That works. Tracker's has helped us out so much over the years. And Abe will be weighing in. I know that his team will be out there searching. That's a given."

"They will be." Caleb paused, running scenarios through his mind. "I can't think of who it would be but it will be the one we least expect. That has been the way it's happened."

"You'll need to talk to Hannah?"

"I will. I intend heading home for a bit over lunch, just to see how the kids are. This is going to go hard on her. Those cousins are close"

"They are." Frankie watched Caleb walk away before he was back at his desk, his programs pulled up as he began to search for the two. He sat back after an hour, not really any further ahead. He hadn't thought that he would find anything but he had to investigate. He was on his feet, his jacket on and heading for his car. There had to be an answer somewhere. And that he needed to find and find rapidly if they were to bring Avery and Kieren home quickly.

Frankie paused as he stopped outside of Mac's diner. Mac would be a good source of information. He turned as he heard his name called and saw Aubrey and Aveleen's husband, Logan, walking rapidly towards him. Just what he needed, he thought, and then asked for forgiveness. He did need to speak with them. Only he had no answers to give them.

Mac watched as Frankie made his way to his favourite booth and shook his head. He's wearing out, he thought. Too many cases involving friends. And now this about Avery? He'll work far too many hours on it.

"Mac?" Frankie looked up as Mac slid onto the seat across from him.

"Frankie? What's this I hear? Avery?"

Frankie nodded, not sure what Mac had heard.

"Avery? Have you any word?" Frankie knew Mac would have heard something or else he would not have sat with him.

"I heard. It's not what that family needs. They've had enough." Mac drew in a breath. "I heard about him early this morning. Not long after it happened, I would think. It was said in passing and I don't know who it was. It was not someone from town."

"Did you get a look at him?"

"At her? No, I didn't. It was as the breakfast crowd was in and it was really busy. I think that she meant me to hear her, but she was in a crowd of people. Strangers to town, if I recall."

Frankie nodded, knowing that Mac spoke the truth. There had been a number of tourists through town that past weekend.

"Thanks, Mac. If you do hear anything, I know that you will pass it on." Frankie sipped at his mug of coffee, looking up with thanks as a plate of food appeared in front of him. "Did you hear anything else?"

"Not really. Although Doug was in here at that time, on his way in. He might have heard something. I suspect that he'll find you if he did." Mac referred to Lieutenant Doug Foster, lead of the ETF and a good friend to Frankie.

"I am sure that he will." Frankie was lost in thought for a moment. "Mac? Have you heard any rumours at all about the radio station? It's just too bizarre."

"Not a thing. And I would. Your street sources would have approached me if they had and they couldn't find you. Streeter is well thought of, he runs a tight ship but given the times and the fact that he is

---

in a niche group for music, he has to. He's always been fair with the employees. I don't know if I have ever heard anything bad about him."

"Nor have I. He's been here for so many years, if something was off, we would have heard about it."

"That we would have." Mac sat for a moment. "You need a vacation, Frankie. You and Deirdre need to get away. Come see me on Friday and I'll give you the key to our cabin for the weekend. You need that time to refresh yourself."

Frankie looked at Mac before he nodded. He had no idea how Mac did it, but he always had a solution for a problem anyone of them faced.

Chapter 5

Aubrey and Logan had hesitated as Mac sat with Frankie, waiting near the door until Mac had risen and returned to the kitchen. They approached and slid into the booth across from Frankie, taking with thanks the mugs of coffee set before them. They knew Mac had seen them and that their favourite meals would appear shortly.

Frankie looked up at them and sighed to himself. He seemed to be sighing a lot lately, he thought. *Mac is right. I do need a break and this weekend works. I'll talk to Deirdre tonight and get her feelings on going away.*

"Frankie? What happened this morning? Where's Avery?" Aubrey finally spoke, his voice broken as he did so. This was his younger brother that had gone missing. It had been bad enough with Aveleen gone and now Avery?

"He's missing. We don't have a lot of information at the moment, Aubrey. Logan. What can you two tell me?" Frankie studied each man in turn.

Aubrey and Logan shared a look.

"I talked to him yesterday afternoon, mid-afternoon. He was just relaxing at home, he said, not really doing anything. He's been wanting a vacation lately, not over what happened with Logan and Aveleen and then myself and Finlee. It took a lot from him. Especially when Logan took that bullet meant for him."

"He has been, Frankie." Logan was troubled. His wife was deeply worried about her brother and had been for days. "Aveleen has been picking up on something but it's nothing definite. We're not sure what has been going on."

"He's restless and has been for a few months. We've talked." Frankie bit into his burger, savouring the taste of the homemade patty. He knew that he needed to eat, even as worried as he was about his friend.

"We know that you can't say much, but someone said the new receptionist is gone as well?" Logan's voice held the questions that he could or would not ask.

"She is. Kitlin MacTavish. We're looking for them, guys."

"But will you find them in time?" Aubrey was on his feet, heading for his home, just to hold his wife, Finlee. He was deeply worried about his brother, not wanting him to go through what he and Finlee had been through.

Frankie watched him walk away before his attention turned to Logan, a frown appearing for a moment as movement outside the window caught his attention. He was on his feet, heading for the young man who was hesitating there. A few quick words and Frankie was heading for his car, more worried than he had been. The young man had simply stated that word on the street was that Avery was mixed up in something illegal but everyone doubted that. They

---

knew the Dennis family and knew that would not happen.

At the end of the day, Frankie sat back, staring at his desk. He was no further ahead, he decided. He had no idea where Avery and Kitlin were. No one seemed to have seen them or whatever vehicle it was that had taken them away. Their families were worried, Avery's parents, Michael and Meg, tracking him down that afternoon. They could give little in way of any information.

Frankie rose, locked his office, and then paced through the building, heading for his car. He needed to speak with someone, only he had no idea who. He paused as he reached the street, finding Eddie Brown leaning against his car.

"Eddie? You're here?" Frankie reached the shake the hand of the retired detective.

"I am. We've heard what happened. Ben is working his sources, looking for information for you. What can I do?"

Frankie leaned against the car, his arms on the roof, deep in thought.

"You know Streeter, Eddie. He's been a member of our church for years. Have you ever heard anything bad about him?"

Eddie had been expecting that very question. It is one which he would have asked, if he had been the investigator.

"Never. He's got a good reputation in town, always ready to help. He's out there on the streets, working with the youth. He told me one time that was where he was when he was their age and someone gave him help, simply telling him to pay it forward when he could. He's been doing that ever since." Eddie squinted at the son. "Timothy's working it as well." Timothy was a close friend of Frankie, as well as Deirdre's cousin and Ben's son. "He looks at Streeter as an uncle."

"I know. This is frustrating. Almost twelve hours and no word."

"It is what it is, Frankie. They disappeared without anyone seeing them. I suspect they are being held close to town. But as to a ransom demand? It depends on who has them and what they want. We may not see that come in for days."

Frankie nodded, Eddie's words echoing his and Caleb's conversation from early that afternoon.

"That's scary, you know. We have no idea who or why, and how do we find them if we don't know that?"

"Leg work. Teamwork. Investigations into them. Emma's weighing in from what she said. She talked with me earlier, just to get names. Not that she needs them."

Frankie cracked a smile at that, knowing that Abe's wife and her team at Tracker's would be looking for their friends.

"Kitlin is new to our town. Not the welcome that she should have received." Frankie turned his head to watch Eddie.

—

"No, it's not. I tracked down her brother at Mac's. Mac called me. He's staying at her apartment, he said, but he really doesn't understand this."

"None of us do. And it is always the one that we least expect who is the ringleader." Frankie nodded as Eddie walked away, his thoughts troubled before he prayed for his friend and the lady with him, asking for protection for the both of them, and a quick resolution to their adventure.

—

Chapter 6

A week had passed since Avery and Kitlin had disappeared from the radio station. Then another three days went by. Frankie was frustrated as were the other investigators from Kitlin's home town. They just couldn't get a handle on where the two were or why they had been taken. Streeter was taking it hard, working Avery's shift at the radio station, his wife covering for Kitlin. It had them all puzzled.

Frankie looked up that day, a frown on his face as the desk sergeant stopped in his doorway.

"Yes, Jesse?"

"Streeter is here, Frankie. He's asking to speak with you."

"Okay, I'll be right out." Frankie took a look at his desk and frowned once more. He was overrun with cases, it seemed, and had been for some time.

He watched Streeter for a moment before he moved through the door to stand beside him, staring out of the window. Streeter stood, his arms folded across his chest.

"Streeter? You needed to speak with me?" Frankie finally spoke when it appeared that Streeter would not.

"I do. Can we walk, Frankie?" Streeter headed for the door, outside and down the steps before Frankie could reply.

Frankie's head dropped for a moment before he was back to his office, grabbing his jacket, and then following Streeter, who had paused just down the street from the station. He drew in a deep breath of the late fall area, the hint of burning leaves wafting to him.

"Streeter? You're here? Why?"

Streeter nodded, his eyes in constant motion.

"I am, Frankie. I know that you can't say where you are in the investigation, but this came today." He held out an envelope. "It's addressed to you but it was delivered this afternoon to the station. Becky found it when she was tidying up before leaving. We don't think that it came with the mail but we're not sure. We don't see anyone coming in or out on the security feed."

"Just staff moving around?" Frankie asked the question that Streeter was afraid to acknowledge.

"That's correct. Becky had not gotten to the mail until then, so it's possible it did come with that. We had a substitute carrier today, not our regular one."

"I see. Have you ever had this carrier before?" Frankie's mind was working on that.

"Never. We know who the carriers are and who covers for whom. This is one Becky didn't recognize." Streeter was quiet as he sat on a bench, his eyes on Frankie.

Frankie nodded, knowing that he would need to follow up yet another lead, a lead that may well go nowhere. He stared at the envelope, seeing the writing

———

in bold black against the white envelope, simply reading Detective Brennan.

"How did they know?" Streeter's question caught his attention.

"Know what? That I'm the investigator? Word is out on the streets. That's how." Frankie reached into his pocket, pulling out a package of latex gloves and pulling out a pair before snapping them on his hands. "Let's see what is in this."

Frankie felt the envelope. It's just not a letter, is it? He could feel objects inside it and that worried him. Opening it carefully, he peered inside. A man's ring. A lady's watch. And a note. He sighed to himself. This meant a trip to the crime lab and more work for an already over-worked team.

"Frankie?" Streeter was puzzled as Frankie just stared at him. "What is in that?"

"A ring. A watch. And a note." Frankie tilted the envelope to study the note. "Whoever it is? They're not saying much. Listen. Can Becky work with a police artist to come up with a sketch of the carrier? He may not be a true employee but then he may be. I'll follow up. Streeter, this is really important what I am asking of you. You need to keep quiet about this. Don't speak to anyone, not even your wife. It could mean Avery's and Kitlin's lives."

Streeter nodded, already coming to that conclusion. His eyes sought the sky, watching the gathering storm clouds. A late afternoon rain was moving in and he feared for his friends, considering

Kitlin a friend as well. He shuddered for a moment before he excused himself and walked away.

Frankie was on his feet, heading for Caleb, finding him in his office working away on his paperwork.

"Caleb? Have a moment?" He stopped in Caleb's doorway, watching as the chief raised his head.

"I do. What do you have?" Caleb waved him in.

"This." Frankie handed over the evidence bags. "Streeter received this. He said that it seemed to be with the mail, but it wasn't their usual mail carrier. I've asked that Becky work with an artist to come up with a sketch for us."

Caleb nodded as he took the bags. He frowned as he saw the ring and watch and looked up at Frankie.

"These are theirs?"

"I believe so. I know that's Avery's class ring from high school. He never takes it off. I would assume the watch is Kitlin's. I'll show Kieren a photo of it and verify that." Frankie's eyes slid closed as he paused to pray. "The note is strange. It doesn't say much at all, does it?"

Caleb looked at the note and frowned. Frankie was right. It was strange and didn't say much. He paused to read it one more.

"We have your friends. And they are not coming home."

Chapter 7

Kieren looked around as he heard running footsteps and stopped his forward walk. Frankie was running towards him, calling for him to wait. A frown appeared on his face.

"Frankie? You're on a mission." He grinned for a moment at his new friend.

"I am. Do you have a moment? I need to go over something with you." Frankie looked around, finally pointing at a local coffee shop. "In there."

Frankie nodded at the waitress as she held up the coffee pot as the men walked by towards a table. He wasn't quite sure how to approach Kieren, not knowing him all that well.

"Frankie? What is it?" Kieren stirred his coffee, watching the detective closely.

"This." Frankie pulled out his phone, found the picture that he wanted, and showed it to Kieren, closely watching his reaction.

Kieren frowned, before his eyes dropped to the photo. His heart froze for a moment before he rubbed at his eyes.

"It's Kitlin's. Dad and Mom gave it to her when she graduated from college. She never leaves it anywhere or lets anyone else wear it. Where did you find it?" Kieren looked up when Frankie didn't respond.

"It was given to someone and they passed it on to us. I can't give details on that as it is part of the investigation." Frankie sighed to himself. They were no further ahead than they had been.

An hour later, Frankie was walking through his old haunts in the downtown area. He had been a street and then undercover officer there for years before he joined the detective squad. He still had many contacts there. Only this time? Not one had come forward to talk with him, to give him the rumours that were rife on the street.

"Frankie?" A low whisper caught his attention and he paused near the doorway of a rundown building. "I know where they are. They're outside of town a bit. Locked up. I don't know who has them but I'm working on that." A slip of paper was slipped into his pocket and the man disappeared into the building, not having really shown himself.

Frankie hesitated for a moment before he walked back towards the detachment building. He waited until he was inside his own office before he reached into his pocket and pulled out the note. He prayed that this would find his friends and bring them home. Only, his experience told him it was not quite that simple.

Staring down at the paper, Frankie drew in a deep breath. He knew that house, had been through it many times on different investigations. Only, he had no way of knowing if they were even still there. He turned to find Caleb, simply handing him the note.

—

Caleb shot Frankie a look before his eyes dropped to the paper. Like Frankie, he recognized the address.

"Have you checked it out?"

Frankie shook his head.

"Not yet. I just was handed that today. I'm heading out there just to scout it out." Frankie hesitated, not sure he was making the right move.

"Take Doug with you." Doug Foster was the head of their ETF squads as well as a good friend to the two men. "He'll want to be involved."

"I was taking of that." Frankie walked away, the piece of paper tucked into an evidence bag and placed on his desk.

"Doug?" Frankie stood in Doug's office doorway, his voice raising Doug's head.

"What's up, Frankie?" Doug sat back in his chair, his pen still in his hand.

"Do you have a few moments? I have an address that I need to check out. Caleb suggested that you go with me."

"Avery?" At Frankie's nod, Doug was on his feet, pen dropped to his desk, a hand reaching for his jacket.

"It's one we've been to before. I don't have enough evidence to get a search warrant, but someone on the street told me that they were there."

"It would be nice to find them today. It's been what a week, ten days?" Doug fastened his seat belt, watching as Frankie punched in his code to get out of the staff parking lot.

"It would be. And it's been ten days. Ten days that their families will never get back." Frankie drove as rapidly as he could to find the address, slowing down and parking away from the driveway. "I think we're okay here. Thank goodness there is not a lot of shrubbery around it."

"No, that is good. They've cleared it up." Doug's eyes were in constant movement. "I don't see a lot of traffic in and out. With the rain, we should do."

"That we would. It looks as if there has only been one vehicle in and out today. That's strange."

"Not really. If they are here, their abductors would not want them to be seen or have it obvious that they are kept here." Frankie moved forward, his jacket open and a hand on his weapon, searching around the house. "I don't see anything overt."

"Nor do I." Doug was frustrated. This was not the first of their friends to have disappeared for days on end. "This has to hurt Avery's people. With Aveleen gone for so long, not once but twice, they don't need to face this with Avery."

"No, they don't. Kitlin's folks are due back tomorrow, Kieren said. I was praying that we would have found them before that."

"And we haven't. Any way to get a warrant to go in?" Doug was grasping at straws, he knew.

—

40

"Not without concrete evidence that they are there." Frankie was frustrated, having to leave without finding out if his friends were actually in the building.

41

The day that they disappeared, Avery had shoved himself against the wall of the van, surprised to find himself among a number of packages. He sighed. This was not how his day was to start. With that thought, he had no idea how it would end, but he was afraid. Afraid for himself and also for the lady with him. He searched in the dark, reaching to find Kitlin's hand. Kitlin jumped as he touched her, a small scream coming from her.

"Kitlin? Did they hurt you?" Avery kept his voice low, even though he was sure that they were on their own. He just didn't know if the men, whoever they were, had monitors in place to keep track of them.

"You scared me!" Kitlin's voice wavered with her fright. "No, they didn't. At least not physically."

Avery felt her shivering and then simply wrapped an arm around her, just as he would his own sister. She stiffened for a moment before she forced herself to relax.

"What now, Avery, is it?" She couldn't see his face in the dark, trying to remember what it looked like. She just couldn't, it had been too brief an encounter between them in the radio station.

"It is Avery. Now, let's see if we can find somewhere to sit. I have no idea where we are heading, but they seem determined to take us somewhere

—

against our will." He gave a grin as she snorted. "Like that, is it?"

"You just had to state the obvious, didn't you?" Kitlin sank to the floor of the cargo area, feeling claustrophobic in the cramped area.

"Did I do that? Sorry!" Avery sat beside her, an arm resting on his upraised knee. He still couldn't see anything, but darkness and that scared him. Not much did that, scare him, he thought. *I can't get out and I need to so that I can get this lady to freedom.*

"Avery? Who were they?" Kitlin's voice was barely audible.

"I don't know. I have never seen them before. And I take it that means you haven't either." Avery drew a deep breath, seeking to pray and finding that very task difficult. He needed to feel God's presence but just couldn't.

"Avery? Why?" Kitlin wasn't sure that he could even give an answer.

"I have no idea. I don't have any enemies, not that I know of. I mean, my sister and brother went through some stuff, but it wasn't directed at me. I just work at the station. I don't have a side gig that's illegal." He had kept this voice low, not sure if they were being monitored at all. "What about you?"

Kitlin shrugged, puzzled by what had happened.

"I don't have any enemies, either. At least, I don't think I do. I was hoping that you could know why." She shrugged, her arm moving against Avery's.

—

She felt safe with him and that she didn't understand. She never felt like that so quickly with anyone.

Avery felt the twists and turns of the van as they fell silent. He could get no sense of where they were or where they were heading. He was afraid, he had to admit to himself, and afraid for his new friend, Kitlin. And he considered her a friend. They were already mixed up in something that scared him. He had prayed that he didn't go through what Aveleen and Aubrey had gone through. It had been too much almost, he thought, to losing them.

The van slowed and moved down a driveway, pulling into a garage and finally to a stop. The men emerged from the cab, standing for a moment to glare at the back door, before the driver headed into the house to find their employer.

The tall and beefy man looked up as the driver approached, his eyes moving to the doorway behind him. The hard, sinful lifestyle that he lived was evident in his face and body.

"Well?"

"We have them both. They're in the van, in the garage. We just need to take them to the cell." The driver waited, knowing that he could go no further until he was given that permission to do so.

The man stared at him for a moment once more and then nodded.

"Do it. Make sure that they don't see the way in. I want them locked up for now. I'll make a decision about what to do with them later. Once you're finished, get back to the cargo company. Come up with some excuse as to why you didn't finish your route. Saul is here?"

"He is. He's in the garage watching the van."

The man nodded.

"Okay. He stays here." The man turned back to his paperwork, not seeing the driver, Theo by name, shoot him a look before he turned and walked away.

Theo hesitated for a moment at the doorway to the garage, suddenly uncomfortable with keeping a woman hostage. And that was what she would be. He had no idea what the plans were for Avery and Kitlin but he feared for them. And he had no idea of how to solve what had just become a huge problem for him.

Saul turned as the door opened, a frown on his face.

"Well?" He waited for Theo to speak.

"He wants them in the cell. How did we end up with a woman? It was only to the guy."

"She was there and saw us." Saul turned to study the door. "I think he knew that all along. Let's get them out and to the cell."

The two men shared a look, neither one wanting to the one who opened the door, but knowing that they had to. A shared thought seemed to be framed in each man's mind. How did they get out of this? Their employer was known to be a vicious, vindictive man. People who worked for him and crossed him disappeared and were never seen again. They feared for their own lives, but also for the consequences of not doing what they were ordered to do.

Chapter 9

The van door rolled up, bringing light into the cargo area. The two men stood, watching as Avery and Kitlin reacted to it, their arms up to shield their eyes.

"Out!" Theo barked at them, angry that he had to tell them that.

Avery rose, a hand out for Kitlin. They dropped down to the garage floor, their eyes on the men. Saul moved behind them, startling them and causing them to jump as blindfolds were dropped over their eyes.

Avery tightened his hand on Kitlin's as they stood for a moment, not sure what was coming, but he knew that they would not be getting away. Not yet, at any rate. A hand roughly grabbed his arm and pulled him away from Kitlin. He heard a whimper from her as he assumed that a hand had found her arm as well. He stumbled as he walked forward, his footsteps echoing on the cement floor of the garage. *Where are we, Lord? And is there an escape route that I can find to get us out of here? I fear for Kitlin, Lord. Please, Lord, protect my new friend. Bring her to safety.*

Kitlin drew in a quivering breath. She was suddenly, deeply afraid. She was in over her head, she thought, but why? That was a question that she could not answer. There didn't seem to be an answer. And the man who had comforted her had not had an answer either.

—

Avery's feet stumbled over one another as a hand came out to brace himself against a wall. He frowned, feeling the roughness of the wall. A tunnel, he thought to himself. A tunnel? Where is it leading us? He could hear Kitlin's footsteps behind him, stumbling as well. *If we are in a tunnel, are we underground or being led to somewhere that would make escaping impossible? And just why? Lord, please help us. Free us.*

The couple was stopped in their tracks and they heard the sound of a lock being opened before they were both shoved forward. Avery hit his hands and knees as he lost his balance. The sound of a lock clicking close came to his ears. His head dropped for a moment as he realized that he would not be able to free himself or free Kitlin. He stayed as he was, waiting for what he didn't know. The only thing that Avery knew was that he and Kitlin were being held captive somewhere and that no one would know where to find them. That scared him, he had to admit.

Kitlin had managed to keep her balance despite the roughness of the shove that had sent her into the room. She waited, for just what she wasn't sure, before she reached for the gag and then the blindfold. She blinked against the sudden light, her eyes squinting until she became accustomed to brightness once more. Searching the room, Kitlin grew more fearful. It was just a room, not overly large with two easy chairs, an air mattress on the floor and a door to one side showing just a small two-piece bathroom. Nothing else. No kitchen. Nothing to say where they were or why.

Turning in a circle, Kitlin began to pray as she had never before. She was on her knees beside Avery, reaching for his blindfold and then the gag, freeing him. She watched as he sat back on his legs, rubbing at his eyes as he too took time to grow accustomed to the light.

"Avery? Are you all right?" Her voice, although pitched low, sounded loud in the room and she winced at that.

"I am. Just shaken up a bit." Avery turned, a hand coming to rest on her cheek. "You're okay? They didn't hurt you?"

"No, just scared me." Kitlin looked around once more before she was on her feet, heading for the door. "It's locked, isn't it?" She pushed at it.

"It is. I heard it lock." Avery was on his feet as well, methodically searching the room and then the bathroom. "There are certainly no comforts of home here, are there? No kitchen. No stove. Just that bit of furniture."

"I don't think we were to be together. I think that they were after you." Kitlin leaned back against the door, her eyes trained on Avery as he paused and then spun to face her.

"Why would you say that?" He walked towards her, stopping feet short of her.

"Because of what the man said when he was dragging me out of the building. He said I wasn't supposed to be there. That you were always on your own in the early morning. And because I was, I had to come with you. They couldn't leave me there to tell what happened."

—

"He said that?" Avery's hand ran through his hair as he stared at the wooden door in front of him, not seeing Kitlin for a moment as he concentrated on the door. "We can't get out. We were taken through a tunnel. It felt like earth under my hand." He spun to stare at the ceiling. "There are no windows. We're underground, I suspect, Kitlin."

Kitlin gave a small sound, not sure if he was correct, but knowing that was likely the answer, she really didn't know how to respond.

"How long will they keep us here?"

Avery gave a grim smile at her question.

"I have no idea. I don't know what they want. I'm not into anything illegal." He paced, his hands jammed into his jeans pockets.

"Nor am I. I came to Riverville because I wanted a change from where I had been living. This is not much of a welcome, you know." She was grumbling but felt entitled to.

Avery gave a grin as he moved to lean on the wall beside her.

"No, it's not, but I'm glad you're in my town. It is a wonderful town. I'll have to introduce you to my friends. They will welcome you."

Kitlin snorted, causing Avery's grin to widen.

"Yeah, about that. If we ever get out of here, I might just move towns again."

―

"Please, don't do that. We need you here in Riverville." At her questioning look, he just shrugged, not sure what else to say.

Chapter 10

Day after day passed for the two, without much contact from their captors. The only time that they saw one of them was in the morning, when a box was dropped off just inside the door. It would hold their food and water for the day. It never varied, food wise. Avery was growing tired of vending machine sandwiches and he suspected that Kitlin was as well.

They had spent time talking the first couple of days, just getting to know one another. Then, Kitlin began to withdraw and grow quiet. She would spend her days curled up in one of the chairs or under a blanket on the mattress. Avery had insisted that she use the mattress, despite her protest and her suggestion that they take turns.

It had been increasingly difficult to tell when it was night or day. The lights never went off or dimmed. Avery was growing tired of that and knew that Kitlin must be as well. He longed to be outdoors, to be free to walk where he chose to. Only that didn't seem like it would happen.

The only variant in their time was the day both men appeared. Avery had been forced to remove his class ring. He heard the whimpers from Kitlin as Saul forcibly removed her watch, despite her protest and pleas not to do that. She had withdrawn even more after that.

—

52

Avery spent much time in prayer, in trying to remember all the verses that he could about safety and protection and resting in God. He knew God was in control, but he still chafed under the bondage that he found himself under.

Kitlin knew that she was withdrawing but could not help herself. She just couldn't, she thought. She was afraid that she would never see her family again or that Avery would not either. He was close to them, he had admitted, even though they had had their difference. She was close with her brother, Kieren, and worried what he would do. He had supported her move to Riverville but still had been saddened that she had moved to a new town. Her parents hadn't said much but she knew that they did support her. Kitlin just wanted them there right now.

"How long has it been, Avery?" Kitlin looked over at him.

Avery was wrapped in a blanket and settled into one of the chairs, where he could watch both Kitlin and the door. He turned to watch her, a frown on his face.

"I'm not sure, Kitlin. At least a week, I think. I can't tell day from night any more." He sighed as he said that.

"Okay. I wasn't sure." Kitlin pulled the blanket tighter around her, her head down on her folded arm. "I'm tired of this. I just want to go home." Her voice held her choked-back tears.

Avery sighed, knowing that he could not do that, take her home that was, as much as he wanted to. He prayed for release but that had not happened. *God,*

*where are You? Please, let us go. Help us to escape
and then find whoever it has been that has taken us
captive.*

Avery dozed off, tired with it all, not sure if he
should sleep but unable to stay awake. He knew that
Kitlin was asleep; he had checked on her not long
before he had sat back down.

A sound at the door roused Avery hours later. He
stared around and then at the door, expecting to see
their food delivered for the day. There was no box,
however. This is strange, he thought. Rising to his
feet, Avery walked around the room, not seeing
anything that would have roused him. He turned to
stare at the door at the end of the room opposite him.

A town on his face, Avery walked to the door, a
hand resting against it for a moment before it dropped
to the knob. Not expecting it to turn, he was surprised
that it turned and then the door opened, stopping as it
came to the end of his reach. Surprise on his face,
Avery stood, staring at the crack that had opened up
before he shoved at the door. It opened all the way,
showing the tunnel that they had been walked through
all those days ago.

Avery stood, shock on his face, knowing that the
way had opened up for them to escape. But was it safe
or a trap? He turned back to stare around the room
before he was over to the mattress, on his knees,
reaching out a hand to shake Kitlin away.

"Kitlin? Come on, Kitlin. Wake up!" He
watched as she stirred, blinking at him/

———

"Avery? What is the problem?" Kitlin sat up, a frown on his face.

"Come on, Kitlin. The door is open. We can get away." He pulled her to her feet, a hand holding hers as she unentangled her feet from the blanket.

"The door?" She stared past him. "How did that happen? And is it safe?"

"I have no idea. I just heard a noise and found it. And I have no idea if it's safe. We need to take care though." He reached for her hand once more, heading for the door, watchful for anything or anyone that might harm them.

They paused at the doorway to the garage, finding it open and wondering at that. They stared at one another, not sure what to expect. Avery moved into the garage, not seeing any vehicles. That didn't matter, he thought. They would walk out. Only he could feel the coldness of the air and they had no jackets. He stood at the door to the garage that opened to the side of it, looking out of it to study the gray clouds. It was early morning, he decided, checking his watch and noting the time.

Kitlin rummaged through the cupboards, searching for anything that they could use. Her hand reached for the two jackets hanging there, snatching them and matching scarves and hats up. She turned to Avery, finding him looking into a backpack, shock on his face.

"Avery?" Her voice was low as she stopped at his side. "Here. I found jackets. And they seem to be the right size for us. And there are boots as well."

"What?" Avery shot her a look and then looked at the jacket and boots that she kept shoving at him. "And this backpack? It's got water and food in it. Someone prepared this for us. Someone wants us to escape."

"They do. Now, can we?" Kitlin's gaze kept shifting between Avery and the door.

"I think so. It's early morning. There doesn't appear to be anyone around. Quick. Into your jacket and boots." He reached for the jacket, shoving his arms into it and zipping it closed, the toque on his head and the scarf wrapped around his neck. He slipped the backpack onto a shoulder.

Kitlin had followed his movements, then walked to the door, peeking out.

"Here, let me have your hand." Avery reached for it and then walked away from the garage, his steps quickening to a run as he headed for the trees near the back of the yard. It had snowed lately, he noted, and he prayed that their footsteps would not be noticed.

Kitlin pulled him to a stop, spinning to stare behind them, her eyes wide.

"Did we really just do that?"

"We did. God opened the door for us and provided for us. We had nothing to protect us or keep us safe from the weather. He provided that." Avery drew in a deep breath. "This is where it gets dangerous, Kitlin. We need to find our way home, and I have no idea where we are."

—

Chapter 11

Making their way slowly through the trees, Avery and Kitlin shivered in the cold air. They could feel the snow in the air and both prayed that they would find shelter and safety before it fell, not sure if they would. Kitlin drew in a deep breath. This was not what she had expected. She was exhausted, she knew, her sleep troubling at best. Avery paused, reaching for a water bottle for Kitlin and then one for himself.

"Did we really just do that?" Kitlin uncapped the bottle and drank, her eyes tracing their steps.

"We did. And we shouldn't have. Someone planned for this."

"Who? Which one of the men?" Kitlin shared a look with Avery.

"I would expect so. Someone developed a conscience. Now, let's see where we are." Avery stared at the sky and then around. "I'm not sure where we are or where we go from here."

Kitlin stared at him, somewhat dumbfounded at his words.

"I thought you did, by the way that you headed this way. You really don't know where we are?"

"No, I don't. I don't recognize the house, but I feel like we're still near Riverville. At least, I pray that we are. That way, our force can investigate our disappearance. I trust my friends there."

—

"Yeah, those friends. They haven't done a very good job of finding us yet." Kitlin was grumbling and they both knew it.

"They had no idea where we were. I don't think we left a whole lot of evidence behind us when we were taken. They'll be trying." Avery reached for her hand, tugging her with him towards where he hoped they could find shelter for the night.

"We need to keep moving, don't we?" Kitlin was puzzled by something. "Avery?"

"What is it?" Avery's eyes were in constant motion.

"Our jackets. They're our size. They were just there in a cupboard along with the hats, scarves, and mitts. That backpack was ready. How?"

Avery turned to watch her face, his head tilting to do so. She's so tiny, Lord. Protect her, please.

"Just like the door was unlocked. That woke me up. We should not have been able to just walk away like we did. Someone helped us."

"I can't see either one of those men doing that. And whoever their boss is sure wouldn't have." Kitlin stopped walking, the tug of her hand stopping Avery, who watched her closely. "An angel?"

Avery shrugged, not quite sure himself what had happened.

"It's possible, I guess. I mean, God can and will do that. I know of a lady, a friend's wife from another town. She had a man who helped her grandmother get away from their town and then he helped her. She could only describe him as an angel. I have heard of others having that happen."

"I see." Kitlin started to walk forward. "Then, if it was, how do we explain how we got away? The door was locked. It's cold and ready to snow. We need to find somewhere to shelter. Too bad we don't have our phones."

"I know. I left mine on my desk at the station. And yours?"

"In my backpack. I never have it out at work." Kitlin grew quiet, worried about where they were and where they were heading. She had forgotten that God was in control and was leading them.

Avery searched for a building or a shelter of some kind and saw nothing. He led them forward, step by weary step, looking for a place to rest. He finally drew Kitlin to a stop near a group of trees, shoving her down onto a log.

"We'll rest here and have something to eat." He reached for her hand, waiting until she had placed hers in his and then bowed his head, praying for protection for them, a shelter for them to rest, and for guidance on how to reach home.

Neither one of them had seen the man, dressed in black, who had stood in the shadows of the garage, his eyes watchful. He had prepared their jackets and the backpack for them, leaving them where the couple would find them. He had also unlocked the door for them and then slipped back to lock it once more to hide their flight. His steps had followed theirs. Only his footprints were not visible.

—

Chapter 12

Avery roused from the doze that he had fallen into, afraid suddenly as he looked around. He drew in a deep breath of relief. They were free, only he had no idea where they were. A sound had awakened him once more. His arm was around Kitlin, keeping her tight to him, in an effort to support her and keep her warm.

A frown on his face, Avery stared down at the ground. A piece of paper lay in front of him. He knew that he had not dropped it. He reached out a tentative hand and retrieved it. The frown deepened on his face as Avery read the words and then studied the map attached to it. Someone had been around when he was sleeping. That scared him. He had not heard a sound. How could he protect Kitlin if he slept like that?

Kitlin roused, pulling the mitten from a hand and then rubbing at her eyes. She frowned in turn as she saw the look on Avery's face.

"Avery?"

"Kitlin? You're awake. We need to move." He held up the paper. "Someone was here and left us a message as well as a map to where we can find shelter for tonight."

"There was? That's bizarre. And we didn't hear this person? Was it our angel?" Kitlin stretched and then was on her feet, pulling Avery up to his. "If that map leads us home and to safety, then I'm all for it."

Avery nodded, heading away from where they had sheltered, Kitlin's hand in his as he holding the paper in the other one. Lord, let this be correct and not another trap. *I need to find shelter for the night. It will be dark soon and I don't want to try and start a fire out in the open. Kitlin needs that, to keep her warm and well.*

The man stood in his study, rage emanating from him as Saul stood in front of him. Saul's face was covered in consternation. He had searched the underground room and couldn't find the couple. The door was locked, and with no windows, there was just no way that they could have escaped. He had been out on his route doing his deliveries, and Theo had been with their boss.

"What do you mean? They're not there. I specifically designed that room for him. And I was assured that there was no way out. Other than the door. And you locked it?" Anger had him almost spitting at him.

"That's correct, boss. There is no way out. I can't explain it. They were there when I checked before I left to do my route." He looked around as Theo tapped and then entered.

"Theo? What is your explanation for this?"

"I don't have one. I don't even see a track where they walked away. And I should. The ground is that wet. They didn't head for the road. It would have been the logical step but I doubt that they would have done that."

—

"Find them. Bring them back. I don't care what condition that they are in when you do." The man turned from his henchmen and back to his desk. Things were happening that no one could explain, and he hated not being in control. Someone would pay for this. And that someone would be Avery.

Frankie looked up as another detective, Jake Wilson, tapped at his door and then entered, sitting down before he handed over a folder. Frankie took it, not quite sure what Jake was up to.

"Frankie? They're not in that house now. Someone got word to Old Joe and he found me at Mac's. They're on the move. Only, I don't know where to or how they are managing." Jake was puzzled.

"They are? That really changes things then. There won't be any evidence that they were in that home then. You're working through the companies that man owns?"

"I am. He owns a lot, quite a few numbered companies. He's been hiding a lot of his activities in them. We'll find what we need and he'll be charged. We just need to find Avery and Kitlin." Jake looked down at his clasped hands. "Aubrey and Logan caught up with me. They've been searching as have Abe's men. They just can't find them. Kieren was around as well. What do we tell them?"

Frankie shrugged, opening the folder and reading through the documentation. Jake's good, he thought. He went right to the heart of it and discovered one of our suspects.

"This is good, Jake. Keep working it. How are your other cases?" Frankie looked up as Jake remained silent. "That bad?"

"It is, Frankie. Why are we so busy? We're having trouble keeping up with the caseload."

"I know. I have talked to Caleb about it. It's not what we wanted. We still think someone is causing this."

"And you would be right." Jake rose to his feet. "I'm off tomorrow. Abe's men are heading out to search and I thought I'd tag along if they'd let me. I spoke with Abe." Abe Finlay had a security team who were good friends with the men.

"That sounds like a plan. Just stay safe. We have no idea what this man is capable of. Not completely." Frankie watched him walk away before his head was bent once more over his paperwork. He rose at last, heading for the outdoors and then a retired officer. *Maybe,* he thought, *Eddie or Ben would have an idea of what to do. I can ask in generalities and find out.*

Chapter 13

Avery looked around, seeking for somewhere dry where they could sit and have a meal. He had searched the pack, finding sandwiches in there. And they were not from a vending machine. Someone had planned this for us, he thought. I need to find that person and thank them. *God, You did this. You are protecting us. Lead us home, please, dear Lord? Protect and heal this lady with me.*

Finding a sheltered area, Avery led Kitlin there and made her sit, reaching for food. His hand hesitated for a moment before he grasped hers and bowed his head to ask a blessing on their food.

Kitlin stared at the sandwich, watching as Avery unwrapped it for her and placed it in her hand. She hesitated to eat, her eyes rising to watch him.

"Eat, Kitlin. Someone prepared this for us. We need to eat to keep up our strength. This map is leading us to where a shelter is for the night. At least, I pray that it does." He bit into his sandwich and chewed, watching the sky. "I think it's going to snow and I want to get us out of the weather before it does."

Kitlin grew quiet, simply eating her sandwich and reaching for a bottle of water. She was puzzled by who had freed them. The two of them had talked about it, neither one coming to a conclusion as to who it might have been.

—

Avery rose and pulled Kitlin to her feet, keeping her hand in his. He knew that she was growing weary, her feet stumbling at times. He was exhausted himself but was forcing himself to keep moving, following the path that had been laid out for them. Avery finally just swept Kitlin into his arms, her head going down on his shoulder as she sighed. Her eyes closed and she slept, exhaustion taking over.

Standing for a moment, his eyes on Kitlin, Avery felt a crack appearing in his heart. He had hardened it years ago, determined that he would never marry, would never love anyone. He had plotted a solitary course for his life, becoming a pauper in love so to say. Even seeing the love between his brother and his wife and his sister and her husband, that had been his determination.

Putting one foot in front of the other, fatigue weighing down his steps, Avery continued to trudge forward. He looked up at the sky, watching as darkness began to fall. He doubted that he would make it to safety before it was completely dark. Only, he had no way of knowing where to find shelter. All he could do was continue his walk, driven by something that he could not explain.

A sound caught at his attention, and Avery paused for a moment. He shook his head. There wasn't anyone out here beside the two of them, now was there? He looked up, to see a ramshackle cabin in his line of sight. Whoever it was who had set them on the right track after all. Shoving open the door hanging by one hinge, Avery entered the cabin, surprised at the neatness and cleanliness of it. He looked around,

———

heading for the couch to lay Kitlin down on it. It was rough and worn, but it was better than the floor. His hand rested on her head for a moment, listening as she gave a sigh and shifted to her side, her eyes still closed in sleep.

Shoving the door closed, Avery looked around, his eyes narrowing as he studied the cabin. He walked to the fireplace, finding a fire already laid, ready to light. He looked around, searching for assurance that they were safe before he shook his head, sighed, and then reached for his packet of matches. His hands held out to the warmth, Avery stood for a moment, still surprised and perplexed that they had been able to just walk away from their captors. He had no explanation for what had happened.

Sinking down beside the couch, Avery leaned back against his, his chin dropping to his chest. He slept as well, his exhaustion allowing him to do nothing else. His sleep was troubled, dreams driving him almost awaken many times. He could see a faceless man chasing them but had no idea who it was.

A sound in the room had Avery on his feet, blinking to drive the sleep away from his eyes. He saw a form in from of him, reaching for him. Instinct drove his actions. His fist came back and he swung at the man in front of him. The unexpected movement caught the man unawares as the fist connected with his jaw and sent him to the floor, where he lay still, a hand on the sore spot.

Avery was wrapped in arms from behind. He struggled to escape but the strength of the man holding him prevented that. An almost sob rose within him as he continued to twist and turn. His ears finally heard the words being spoken, that the men were friends, and would he just stop for a moment so that they could talk? His struggles began to stop and he stood, the arms dropping from around him. A hand rested on his shoulder and he turned his head, to find his friend, Murphy O'Brien, standing there.

"Murphy? What? How?" Avery looked around that point, seeing five of Abe's security team as well as Jake Wilson. "Jake? Matt? Ian? Luke? Joseph? How? And where are the rest of you?"

"Micah is in our van. Abe and Nathaniel are outside, scouting out the area. Now, we need to move you two and now." Murphy was puzzled. "But how did you get here? The last we heard you had disappeared."

Avery sighed, knowing that he had to give a statement but wanting to get Kitlin to safety.

"Jake? I don't know why you're here, but we will talk. Can we get Kitlin out of here?" Avery staggered as he moved, only Murphy's hand on his arm keeping him upright.

Matt had moved to assess Kitlin, kneeling beside the bed. He was the paramedic on the team. He turned for a moment as Avery staggered, his eyes assessing him.

"Can you manage him, Murphy?" Matt's question was quiet. They were all speaking in low tones, even though they appeared to be on their own there. They had no idea where the men were who had trapped the couple.

"We can. Let's get a move on." Murphy reached once more to tuck a hand under Avery's arm even as Ian moved to do the same on his other side. The two men shared a look before heading out.

Matt simply gathered Kitlin into his arms, watching her face as she didn't stir. That concerned him, not knowing what the two had been through. Luke grabbed for the backpack even as Joseph extinguished the fire. Jake had moved out already, his steps following the men in front of him. He had no cell service right now, that he knew, but he would be in touch with Frankie and Caleb just as soon as he did have. He had not really expected to find the couple even though Abe was sure that he knew just where they were. Jake knew that he would be asking Abe how he was so sure.

Chapter 14

Avery wrapped his arm around Kitlin once more. Safely buckled into Abe's large passenger van, he felt safe once more, or reasonably safe, he thought. His eyes on Kitlin as she slept, he grew afraid once more. They had escaped or been released, but that didn't mean that they were safe.

Abe studied him before he shared a look with Matt. Matt simply shook his head, not having had a good chance to assess either one of them.

"Avery?" Abe waited until Avery looked at him. "Were you mistreated in any way?"

"No, that's the strange thing. We were locked in a room underground. We had meals and water delivered every morning. This morning? The door wasn't locked and we could simply walk out. These jackets and that backpack? They were waiting for us. Then, when we had stopped for a rest, a map appeared in front of me, leading us to that cabin. I don't get it."

The men in the van exchanged glances. This was not what they had expected to hear. Jake reached for his phone, finding that he had service, and sent a text message to Frankie, simply stating that they had the couple and were heading into the hospital with them. Would he meet them?

Frankie stared at his phone, not quite believing what he was reading. He was on his feet, searching for Caleb, finding him in the break room.

—

"Caleb? Jake just sent a message. Abe's men found Avery and Kitlin."

Caleb spun, not quite believing what he was hearing.

"What did you say?" He reached for Frankie's arm, spinning him around and sending him back through the door and to Caleb's office.

"Jake sent a text message. They have Avery and Kitlin. They are on their way in. He didn't say much more." Frankie sank into a chair, still in shock that the couple were found.

"That's interesting. Head over and meet them." Caleb looked up at that, his eyes trained on the door. "We'll need to call their families. Kieren is still in town, I know, and has medical power of attorney for Kitlin. Her parents are heading this way today, he told me yesterday. I'll find Michael and Meg and send them in for Avery. They'll call Aubrey and Aveleen." Caleb's mind was racing. "We need officers on their doors. Abe said yesterday when we talked that they were available for today but all of the team was involved in training tomorrow."

"I know." Frankie stood, hesitation in his movements. "How did they get away? And where were they the whole time?"

"That we'll find out when we get their statements. How long before they're here?" Caleb waited as Frankie pulled up another text from Jake.

"About fifteen minutes, he thinks. They weren't that far away, from what he said. Apparently they were kept in an underground room." Frankie looked up at Caleb's gasp of surprise. "Caleb?"

"You know, I heard that there had been an underground room built somewhere. Just rumours, I thought. I guess not after all. On your way. Call me when you get more details. And send Jake in to work on this. I'll talk to him about his other cases. We will not let any slide just to look into this."

Frankie walked through the Emergency department, looking for Jake, finding him standing near the ambulance bay doors. Jake turned as he heard the footsteps, pointing to the outside. Frankie handed over the cup of coffee he had been holding for Jake.

"Talk to me, Jake. What happened?"

Jake was shaking his head.

"It's bizarre. We found a cabin and saw the smoke. Some of Abe's men went in and I followed. They were there, sleeping. Avery can't explain what happened to get them there. He simply stated that the door to the room was unlocked, that jackets and a backpack were waiting for them, and that a map was left in front of him leading them to the cabin. That cabin? It was on the outskirts of town. Avery thinks that they walked most of the day, but he didn't know where he was. He hadn't recognized the area. Which is not surprising, considering where we found them."

"Do we have a name yet?" Frankie was hopeful, his eyes watching the traffic around them.

———

"Not yet. He hasn't been able to give us anything yet. The doctors are with them." Jake sighed. "We need to speak with the families."

"And we will. Abe's are still around?"

"They are. They'll stay for now, he said, but then have to leave." Jake turned back into the department. "I have their statements. Kitlin was awake enough to give that. Their families are around."

"I gathered that they would be. Did we learn anything about who it was?"

Jake shook his head, puzzled at that

"No, we didn't. But Avery did say that it was a delivery van that they were shoved into. They had been surrounded by packages."

"That we didn't know. You're working that angle?" Frankie paused at the doorway to a room, his eyes on Kitlin and Kieren.

"I am. Caleb called and asked that I come back in. I'm heading in with their statements and to see what I can come up with." Jake walked away, Frankie watching him before he moved into Kitlin's room.

"Kieren?"

Frankie's voice brought Kieren's head around and he rose to come to stand beside the detective.

"Frankie. Thank you for finding them. She isn't saying much, wanting to sleep. She won't say anything. I know her."

"It was Abe's team that found them. I didn't do anything. Nor did Jake. And she will speak with us.

That's a given. She won't have any choice." Frankie waited for a moment and then turned and walked away, heading to find Avery.

Chapter 15

Frankie walked towards Avery, finding him sitting on the side of the bed in the examination room, his eyes on the floor. He had slept for a while, been assessed, and was told that he could leave. Only Avery didn't want to leave. He wanted to stay where Kitlin was. He worried about her, worried about what would happen to her when they were apart.

Avery finally raised his head, his eyes on Frankie. He sighed to himself. He would need to speak with Frankie. Only, he had no idea what to say.

"Avery? What else can you tell us?" Frankie leaned against the bed, watching Avery closely.

Avery shrugged, not willing to say much.

"I don't know, Frankie. I never saw the men's faces. The van? It was a delivery vehicle with actual packages inside but I don't remember seeing any name on it. But then we were shoved in from the back and couldn't see the sides of it. Kitlin and I spoke. Neither one of us have any idea who they were. How is she?" Avery watched Frankie's face, seeing it shuttered.

"She's sleeping right now. And then Kieren will take her back to her apartment. Her parents are in town and heading that way instead of here." Frankie looked around as he heard footsteps and Michael and Meg, Avery's parents, appeared. "And here are your parents."

Michael and Meg hugged their son, their worry somewhat relieved but not totally gone. Michael shared a look with Frankie.

"Thank you, Frankie, for bringing our kids home." Michael stood, an arm around Meg. "Aveleen and Aubrey are waiting outside. Can we take him home?"

"You can. But not to your home, Mom and Dad. I want to go to my own home. I need that." Avery was off the bed, walking away from them, heading for Kitlin. He just needed to see her and assure himself that she was okay.

Aubrey walked beside his brother, Aveleen on his other side, an arm linked with his. Neither sibling spoke to their brother, knowing how they had felt during their adventures as they were called.

Kieren turned as he felt a presence beside him, a frown on his face at the man standing here, a hand reaching out to rest on Kitlin's face. He looked behind him at the man and lady standing behind him. The faint sounds of the busy Emergency ward caught at his ears.

"You're Kieren?" Avery phrased it as a question, but he knew the answer. "I'm Avery."

"I am. Thank you for getting her away from those men." Kieren hesitated before he reached to draw Avery into a hug.

"I just led her from the room, but someone else opened the door for us and left us supplies. I want to find that person and thank them." He looked around at the room, still not believing that they were free. "You're taking her home?"

"I am." Kieren handed over a slip of paper. "This is her address and her phone number. Mom and Dad are there. They'll want to speak with you. Call us tomorrow and we'll get you two together. You both need that contact with one another. You have been through something together which requires you have that contact with one another. We'll talk, Avery. Call me tonight and see how she is."

Avery walked away after a few moments, leaving behind the lady who had become a huge part of his life. He didn't want to but he had to. He prayed hard for his lady as he had begun to think of her in his heart of hearts, not wanting to acknowledge it yet.

Aubrey watched as Avery walked away, his arm around his sister. He knew that Finlee and Logan were waiting for them as were their parents but for now? He just needed to stand there and pray for his brother. He knew how he had felt when Aveleen had been in danger. He could get how Avery now felt after being in danger himself. But each adventure was unique. Only God and their faith in Him would get them through this. That he was confident of.

Avery wandered his home that night, not sure what to do. It felt odd being free once more. The underground room had consumed their lives for so many days, ten he was told, and that was something that he could just not set aside. He had spoken with Streeter, who was relieved that Avery and Kitlin were free. His only question had been what could he do for them? Avery had given a bark of laughter and then sighed, swallowing against the tears in his throat. He had been unable to speak for a moment, his eyes on the fire which he had lit in the gas fireplace.

"I really don't know, Streeter. I really don't know. Are you in tomorrow?"

"I am. Come in when you're able to and we'll walk through the building. I had Joseph come through and up our security. The way we work now has changed. Everyone has agreed to that. No more unlocked door at the front. There is a box for parcels and the mail to be delivered to, locked from the inside. I want it to be as safe as I can for you and Kitlin."

"Thank you, Streeter. That means a lot. I'll see you at some point in the morning. I'm not sure about Kitlin though."

Streeter gave a laugh, having already spoken to Kitlin.

"She's coming in around 10. How be you come at the same time? She is adamant that this person as she calls him will not win. She wants to take back this part of her life, and I agree with her. You both need to."

Avery had set his phone on the counter, walking away from it. It had been chiming almost without stop since he arrived home. He had spoken with his parents and his siblings, assuring them that he was okay and just needed a few hours to get his head on straight again. He had read the text from Kitlin, a smile on his face as her words. *Yes,* he thought, *I am okay, sweetheart. And I am glad that you are free as well and home. We'll talk and soon. I will see you on the morrow, and I can't wait for that. I just need to think about how to keep you safe.*

Kitlin turned over in bed, drawing the covers up almost over her head. The hot shower had helped to warm her. It had been good, she thought, to do that and get into clean clothes. She heard Kieren moving around and the quiet conversation from her parents before the apartment quieted down. She hadn't said much, but then her family had not questioned her, only hugging her and holding on for a while. They were close. Kitlin was glad that they were here. She didn't think that she could handle tonight being on her own. Avery had become a big part of her life in the last few days and she missed him. His text answering hers had brought a smile to her face. He is such a caring, compassionate man. *Lord, protect my friend. Don't let him be hurt any more.*

Chapter 16

Avery stood at the back door of the radio station, hesitant to enter. The fear of being abducted again drove through him. He didn't hear the footsteps that stopped beside him, jumping as he felt a hand on his shoulder and then Abe's prayer. Abe had known how hard it would be for him and had wanted to be there for him.

"Avery? It's hard, I know. We'll walk you through this."

"You're not supposed to be here. You have a team in for training." Avery was grateful, however, for his friend being there.

"Right now, you need a friend here. Emma's working away on what she can but has had some urgent work that she needed to work on first. She's getting there." Emma, Abe's wife, had a company that tracked people, finding them when other authorities couldn't.

"Thank you. I need to go in, but it's hard." He reached for the door, finding it opening before he could touch it. He jumped.

Streeter stood there, Kitlin just behind him. He gave a grim smile at Avery's look of shock.

"It's okay, Avery. Let's get you in and out of sight. Then I can explain the new security system to you. We'll be making changes to our schedule as well, if we need to."

"That's not necessary, Streeter. We will work with what we have to." Avery listened carefully as Streeter explained the new system, signing in with a new password. "This looks good, Abe."

"Joseph was adamant that he do this. He spoke with another security expert that he's friends with just to run it by him."

"That's good." Avery moved towards Kitlin, ignoring the two men with him. "Kitlin? You're okay?" He watched as conflicting emotions chased one another across her face.

Kitlin shrugged, not sure how to respond.

"I'm okay, I guess. And you?"

"About the same." He simply reached to hug her and then turned her to face into the building, keeping his arm around her. He felt her leaning into him. "Streeter? What other changes are there?"

"A lot. Abe here can explain what security changes we have made. We want to keep you two safe as well as anyone else here. Abe?"

Abe nodded, pointed to the studio.

"We can't go in there yet, but we have set it up so that you can lock yourself in there. There is a panic button set up that connects directly to the security company. If you hit it, they will immediately call the authorities. If that panic button goes off, all the doors to the building will be locked and only opened for a certain code. That code is only available from the security company. That's how Streeter wanted it. And before you ask, Emma and Jace have researched the company and everyone connected with it. You're safe that way.

"Now, the offices. The same sort of ability to lock yourselves in and with panic buttons as well. They went after you, Avery, but it could have been anyone of you. Now the reception area. Kitlin, you were concerned about that. You told Streeter that. He has taken that into account as well. The main door is kept locked. No one can enter without an appointment, and those appointments will be vetted for you for now. Gideon, my brother-in-law, is an investigator and has agreed to do that for Streeter. His old boss is on board with that too.

"There is a panic button near your desk, Kitlin. The mail and packages will be delivered to a box outside the office, which connects to the reception area with a locked door. It can only be opened from inside and is not large enough for anyone to get through." Abe's gaze flickered between the two of them. "Do you have any questions?"

Avery shook his head, his own eyes on Kitlin, who was staring at her desk before she sat.

"What about the phone system? How secure is that?"

"As secure as we can make it. We've changed it somewhat, but there will be cell phones, fully charged at all times, kept in every room, including the break room. I hate that we have to do this, Avery, but it is a necessary step. We don't know who it was that abducted you or why. We're looking at digital piracy, but so far, we haven't had any confirmation on that.

—

We will keep you two in the loop, as we say, about that. Frankie is adamant that we give him anything that concerns any one of us."

Avery nodded before he moved to crouch down beside Kitlin, an arm resting on the chair arm.

"You're okay? You feel safe here?"

Kitlin finally nodded.

"I do, but I'm still scared, Avery. They can still get us when we're away from here." Kitlin didn't want to admit that she had was scared that he would disappear on her.

Avery nodded before he began to pray, his prayer bringing them to God's throne and calming her fears.

"We sometimes feel that we have nothing left to give and that we are alone. We are never alone. God is here with us all the time. And we do sometimes feel like paupers, depleted of everything. And we shouldn't. God understands that, Kitlin. We need to make a pact between us, that we will meet for prayer and Bible study when we are not at work. And I have friends whose wives will speak with you and meet with you. Without even having met you, they have offered to do that."

"They have?" Kitlin had turned her head to watch him. "You have wonderful friends."

"And they want to be your friends as well. Now, let's see what mischief we can get into here for now and then I want to meet your folks. I met Kieren last night."

—

Kitlin eyed him, not quite sure what he was meaning, but sure that he would tell her at some point.

83

Late that afternoon, Avery stood in Kitlin's apartment, shoulder to shoulder with her brother. They faced Kitlin, who stood, arms wrapped around herself as she glared at them. Avery kept his grin hidden, but Kieren was not so kind to his sister. His grin was open on his face and his eyes twinkled with mischief. He could see her parents, Esther and Paul, standing behind her. Her mother had a look on her face that said not to tease but her father was grinning as well.

"It's okay, Kitlin. I understand." Avery reached to pull her into a hug, ignoring the looks shot at him. "You're scared. You just came home from an abduction. And you're not sure if you're safe anywhere."

"You understand?" Kitlin looked up at him.

"I do. I feel the same way. Aveleen and Aubrey had said the very same. Only Aveleen was missing for four months at first and then for a couple of months. In fact, when her husband and I were out looking for her, he took a bullet meant for me."

"He did?" Paul spoke up, not being aware of the history.

"He did. He didn't walk for a while but when Aveleen was assaulted in front of him, he just stood and ran for her." He looked around, assessing the three with him. "Now, we need to eat and make some plans."

"We do. Only I don't know that I have any edible food here." Kitlin moved away from him, not wanting to but knowing that she needed to. She needed to put space between them, still unsure of her feelings for him or his for her.

"We shopped for you this morning when you were at work, Kitlin." Esther moved to wrap an arm around her daughter. "Dad wanted to do that. Now, what shall we have? I did put a roast in the oven earlier, but if you want something different, we can do that."

"As long as you make your Yorkshire pudding, I'm good with that. What do we need to do now?" Kitlin moved into the kitchen, reaching for plates to set the table. She turned as her mother stopped, not sure what was going on.

"I am just so glad that you are home, Kitlin. It really worried us that we weren't here at first. Dad wanted to leave his job and come home."

"I'm glad that he didn't. There wasn't anything that he could have done, not really. Do you think this has anything to do with Dad's work?"

Esther hesitated for a moment. She and Paul had discussed that and talked with Frankie, who agreed that it might have, but that it didn't include Avery. It seemed as if he was the target, not Kitlin, although they couldn't rule out that totally.

"We talked with the detective. He agreed that it could, but that wouldn't explain Avery being kidnapped."

—

85

"This is frustrating, Mom." Kitlin stared around her kitchen. It was large enough to have her table in it. She loved the soft yellow it was painted in and the two tone cabinets. It was a kitchen that she could see herself spending time in.

"We know, Kitlin. We know. It's frustrating for all of us." Esther shot a look towards the doorway, hearing the three men's voices coming from the living room. "What really happened? You didn't say much last night."

"It's so bizarre. We were taken from work, shoved into a cargo van, and then walked into an underground room. It was only one room with hardly any furniture. No kitchen. Only a two-piece bathroom. Avery worried about me. I could tell that. Then yesterday, he woke me up. The door had been unlocked. There were jackets and winter stuff waiting for us in a cupboard in the garage. There was a backpack with food and water. We just walked away. And then when we were taking a break, I think we both dozed off. Avery woke up to find a map and directions to shelter on the ground in front of him. That's where Abe and his team found us. Who does this?"

"I would say that God did."

"That's what I think. I think we had a guardian angel going this. Is that even possible?" Kitlin felt her father's arm around her shoulders. "Dad? Isn't that what you always say?"

"It is, love. It is. It is entirely possible that it was an angel. Or else someone who knew where you were and took advantage of you two being there on your own to get you away. You just need to be very careful." Paul looked around as they all gathered in the kitchen. "We need to keep you two in constant prayer."

Avery walked away later that evening, heading for home. He had walked, needing the time to clear his head, not even thinking about the danger that he might be in. He didn't hear the running footsteps behind him until he was facedown on the sidewalk, the knee in his back not letting him rise. He had slammed down abruptly, the force of the fall taking away his breath. Hauled to his feet, Avery struggled as best that he could to escape but was unable to free himself from the hands holding him in a tight grasp.

"You've been warned. You will cooperate with us. When you least expect it, we will come after you. You will not see us around you, but you will be watched constantly. And your woman? We're watching her too."

A fist was driven into Avery's abdomen, doubling him over and dropping him to his knees. A blow to the back of his head dropped him to the sidewalk once more. Avery didn't move as the men moved away, their running footsteps sounding loud in the stillness of the night. The snow that had begun to fall drifted down through the stillness of the early December night, melting as the flakes first hit his body and then beginning to cover him.

A man out for a late night walk with his dog hesitated as he saw the body in front of him before he was on his knees beside Avery, a hand out to check for a pulse. His phone out, he called for help, rising to

—

watch as the blue and red lights of the emergency services converged on his location.

Dave Allison, the paramedic who had responded, sat back for a moment, surprised to find that it was Avery. He had not heard that Avery had returned home. He shared a look with his partner, Tom, who nodded.

Standing at the back of the paramedic rig, Dave spoke with the responding officer, who nodded and pulled out his phone. Frankie would need to be advised. Only they couldn't talk with Avery. He was still unconscious.

—

Chapter 18

Frankie strode through the hospital parking lot. He had been working late, as the on call detective, when the call had come in to him. He had shaken his head and then risen, reaching for his heavy winter coat and walking rapidly to his vehicle. What more can happen to these two, he wondered? And then he sighed. He remembered what it had been like for him and his wife, Deirdre, what they had faced and how close to death they had been.

The physician treating Avery looked around and nodded. Frankie stood to the side, watching closely. The physician, John Thompson, a man from their church, swung his stethoscope around his neck and then moved to stand beside Frankie.

"What can you tell me, John?"

"He was beaten, Frankie, although not severely. His abdomen is soft. There is also a lump on his head where I suspect he was struck. It's the exposure that has us concerned. Given what he just went through, it could well be a factor. He's lost weight from what had happened in the past two weeks."

"He has. Anything else?"

"No, I don't think so. We'll keep him overnight here in Emergency. His father is on his way in."

"Okay. I guess that means I don't get to speak with him yet. Leave word for me that no one questions

—

him until one of us speaks with him. I'll be around early in the morning. If he isn't awake by then, Jake Wilson will be here. We need to find out what happened to him and if he knows who did it." Frankie walked away, back to his vehicle, where he stood, staring at the accumulating snow before he looked up. He just couldn't catch a break with this case. And if he didn't soon, it would be set aside for the time being. He had other pressing cases on his desk.

Kitlin stared at Streeter the next morning as she stood in his office at the radio station, shock on her face.

"I don't understand. I thought that you just said that Avery was in the hospital. He was fine when he left my place last night. He had dinner with me and my family." Stress coloured her face.

Streeter nodded to himself. There's interest there, all right, he thought. Only she won't say anything until Avery does.

"He was attacked on his way home. He was walking, Kitlin. Do you understand the risk that he put himself in?" At her nod, he sighed. "I spoke with his father. He's still in the hospital and not awake as yet. He was knocked out and then spent some time out in the elements."

Kitlin's face paled at that. She had had no idea that he had been walking.

"I didn't know. Dad would have given him a ride home. Or Kieren would have. Why didn't he say anything?"

"That's who Avery is. He doesn't want to put anyone out or cause any trouble for anyone. He's trying to take care of you, Kitlin. That's obvious with how he is reacting." Streeter didn't say that Avery had talked with him the day before, stressing that Kitlin needed to be safe. And asked him how they could do just that.

"I see." Kitlin paced, her arms wrapped around herself. She studied the lunch room, taking in the white refrigerator, the microwave, the light brown cupboards, and the coffee maker and teakettle. "I can't have him putting himself at risk to do that."

"It's not going to be your choice, Kitlin. It's what he has determined to do. We can't stop him. I know him well enough to know that. Now, how do we do that?" Streeter pointed to the door. "Let's get you at your desk, and then go from there. I think we have done as much here as we can. We need to find someone to be out and about with you. For now, we have offers from the police force for officers to drive you back and forth to work. I have accepted that. There are also offers for them to be with you when you need to be out and about, if you don't have anyone with you."

Kitlin stared at him, not sure what to say. She sighed, bringing a smile to his face.

"I guess. I hate putting anyone at risk."

"You're not doing that. It's what they do, as officers. These are ones who are volunteers. They know the Dennis family and want to help. They don't want to see you and Avery go through what his siblings did."

Kitlin sighed once more.

"I thought that's what you would say. We did talk, Avery and I. I know what happened to his sister and brother and how his brother-in-law was shot in his place. I just don't know. I worry about my family. Will they go after them to get to me?"

"That we don't know yet. We don't know why you were taken, other than that you were here. Avery seems to have been the target all along. Only we don't know why."

Kitlin stared at him before she looked around the reception area. She stared at the picture on the wall, that of a stream running through a forest.

"Streeter? Why? What would they want?"

"I have an idea that I am looking into. Music piracy is a big problem now. That could be one of the things that they are after. We are looking at other things as well."

"Does someone want to take over the station? Is it that profitable?" Kitlin was thinking aloud.

"We've had offers over the years, but I have always turned them down. I am not ready yet to give it up. And when I do, I know who I will offer it to. Now, let's see what we can accomplish today. If you need me, I'll be in my office. Don't hesitate to come and find me."

Streeter stood where he could watch Kitlin. She was upset, he could tell, and he knew that she wanted to flee the station and find Avery. But she would stay at her desk until her work was done. He shook his head. He could see Avery and Kitlin as a couple. Only would they survive to become that?

Chapter 19

Avery shifted on the hospital bed, not quite sure what had happened. His eyes closed against the light, his headache worsening. He had not planned on being here. He had planned on being at work. Only that wasn't happening, not today. Avery didn't look around as he heard footsteps approaching his bed and stopping.

"Avery? What did you go and do?" Aubrey stood there, Finlee beside him.

"I have no idea. I can remember walking away from Kitlin's place and then waking up here." He squinted at them. "What did I do?"

"Apparently, you were attacked on your way home. Someone walking their dog found you." Aubrey shared a look with Finlee. "You were unconscious when you were brought in."

"I know. Jake was around and took my statement. That's why we can talk." Avery shifted once more. "When can I go home?"

"Today. But they want someone with you."

"That's not happening. And I'm not going to either one of your places. Or to Mom and Dad's."

"That's what we thought you would say. They'll let you go home, but you have to have someone with you for a few hours. That's not an option." Aubrey knew his younger brother and knew that he would kick at that.

"Not one of you. You both have to work." Avery looked past Aubrey, seeing Kieren hesitating in the doorway. "Kieren will stay with me."

"I will, Avery. That's why I'm here. Well, part of the reason. Kitlin wants to see you when she's finished work and that means she gets to see you at your place. Dad will bring her."

"And my parents will be there. I just know it." Avery's eyes closed and then he slept, leaving the three with him to exchange amused glances.

Four hours later, Avery sank onto his couch, grateful to be home. Kieren took his jacket and headed for the hall closet to hang it up. He could hear the soft conversation from the kitchen, knowing that both sets of parents were there. He turned to the door as he heard a soft tap, opening it to draw his sister into his hug.

"He's here, Kieren?"

"He is, Kitlin. He's sore and unsteady on his feet. I'll stay overnight with him. Mom and Dad are with you." He looked around. "Avery's parents are here as well. I just hope that we don't overwhelm him." Kieren stared down at his sister. "How was work?"

Kitlin shrugged, not quite sure how to respond.

"It was okay. Busy. I'm trying to learn a new job under circumstances that are difficult. Streeter is a great boss. He's arranged for someone to escort me back and forth to work for now. He said officers have volunteered. They want to do that for the Dennis family."

"And for you, as well. They want to see this resolved for you both." He turned Kitlin and then shoved her towards the living room. "Go find your fellow, sis. He's in there and waiting for you."

Kitlin bit at her lip, not sure why Kieren had worded it that way, but she moved towards Avery, finding his hand out to grasp hers and pull her to a sitting position beside him. His arm wrapped around her and caught her close to him. Kieren blinked for a moment, seeing his beloved younger sister falling in love in front of his eyes and glad for that. He felt his father's arm around his shoulders.

"She's okay?" Paul's voice was low.

"She is." Kieren bit at his lip. "She's falling in love, Dad."

"She is, son. And we could not have picked a better man for her. I've spent time with his parents, his siblings, and his friends. They all speak highly of him. But most importantly, he is a man of God, an honourable man who will love your sister and treat her as she should be treated, a precious jewel, which she is."

"That he will." Kieren hesitated for a moment. "Now that you're home and retired, Dad, where are you and Mom going to live? Kitlin isn't leaving this town. And I am thinking of moving here. I've been really restless at home lately."

—

"We know you have, son. We like this town as well. Perhaps we'll settle here. Michael is trying to persuade us to do that. It's a big decision."

"It is." Kieren turned as Michael appeared at his side. "Michael, how many lawn care companies are there in town?"

Michael laughed, knowing what Kieren was asking without saying it.

"There is a number but there is always room for more. You would be welcome here, Kieren. We have a young friend who dedicates his company to those who are seniors. What we need is someone who can help the single mothers and those who are handicapped. Most companies avoid them as they don't make a lot of money off them. I can put you in contact with Timothy and he'll be happy to help you get set up here."

"That would work." Kieren watched his sister, wrapped in the arms of a man who was clearly falling in love with her. "Kitlin isn't leaving here, and Mom and Dad will likely move here."

"That they will." Michael watched as Paul moved away at a call from his wife. "Your father is restless and has been."

"He is. And Mom is too. She volunteers with a shelter at home when she can but they've been overseas now for a couple of years. I know that she misses that."

"We'll find something for them to do. Now, Kieren, what are your thoughts about what these two are going through?"

Kieren shrugged, not quite sure what Michael was asking.

"I haven't really had much time to think about it. I can do that. I have a journal that I started with Kitlin disappeared."

"That helps. Let me put you in contact with Emma, Abe's wife. She's working on it as she can. And there are a couple of retired officers who would be good for you to speak with. In fact, Eddie and Ben and their wives are to come for dinner tomorrow night. How be you and your parents join us?"

"I guess." Kieren watched as Michael walked towards his son, a hand out to rest on Avery's head.

Chapter 20

Kieren closed the door slowly behind his sister, having watched as Jake walked her to his car. She was heading home, even though she didn't want to. He could hear Avery moving around, his steps slow. He turned and headed for the kitchen, stopping for a moment to stare around and then reaching for the dishes to start cleaning the kitchen from their meal.

Avery reached for the coffee pot, pouring both of the men mugs of coffee. He turned, more steady on his feet. His headache was fading but it was still there enough for him to be aware of it. He had no idea why he was attacked, and Jake had not been able to give much more information. As far as he could remember, they hadn't asked him for anything.

"Kieren? You don't have to do that." Avery gave a low groan as he sat at the table.

"I know, but they need to be done." Kieren reached for his mug of coffee, the dish towel thrown over his shoulder. "How much do you remember?"

"Not a lot. I know that they didn't ask for anything. At least, that's what I think they did. Just warned me. But it's so bizarre. Why me? I don't have any enemies. At least, I don't think that I do."

"Someone wanted something from you or wanted you to do something." Kieren tucked the towel back on the stove door. He reached for the pad of paper and pad laying on the counter and sat himself down at

---

the table. "Let's do some brainstorming before you head for bed."

Avery gave a slight nod, knowing that any further movement would make it worse.

"Okay, we can do that. What do we start with?"

"Start with all the people who work at the radio station. Then move out from there to suppliers, couriers, mail people." Kieren's pen scratched across the paper. He sat back at length, his eyes on Avery.

"There are not many here, Kieren. I don't seem to make enemies." Avery sighed, raising his mug to drink at his cold coffee. "There has to be something."

"There is. But for now, you need to get some rest. When are you heading back to work?"

Avery shrugged, not sure of that anymore.

"Monday. Today is Friday, so that gives me a couple of days to recover." Avery stood, a finger rubbing along the back of his chair. "Kieren, you're welcome to stay here for as long as you want. You're thinking of changing towns?"

"I am. Kitlin is here. Mom and Dad are thinking of moving towns now that he's retired. That had been their plan for years. Only, they didn't have a town in mind."

"Until now. I'd welcome the company." Avery walked away, his steps steadier than they had been.

Monday morning found Avery standing in front of the back door to the station, the sun not barely visible. He felt the fear once more from what had happened. Ian stood beside him, Micah with his back to them. They had been the volunteers that morning who had appeared at his door to escort him to work.

"It's hard, isn't it?" Ian's voice was quiet. "Let's get you inside and settled to your task."

"It's okay, Ian. I'll get there, I know. It is just hard, the not knowing who it was."

"It is, Avery. Your siblings can tell you that. We can all tell you that. You know our stories, what happened to us." Ian closed the door behind them, Micah remaining outside. "Now, Kitlin is here already. We have been asked that the two of you work the same hours. It makes it easier for security during the day."

"It would. It's the outside-of-work hours that we need to worry about. We can't be together all the time. I can feel them watching us every day, every hour, Ian. How do we find them? Kieren and I made a list on Friday night with everyone we could think of. I passed that on to Jake and Frankie. Emma has a copy. If you want a copy, I'll get it to you."

"That would help, Avery." Ian's eyes had raised to the hallway, seeing Kitlin standing there, hesitant about entering the office. "Here's Kitlin."

Ian walked away, a hand on Kitlin's shoulder for a moment before he gave her a small push towards the office. Avery stood in the doorway, watching her, and then reaching to draw her into his hug.

"Okay, sweetheart?" He felt her nod against him. "Okay. I know the phones don't open for a bit.

Sit here and help me pick out the music for today. I have a sort of list, but can always change."

"What do I have to do?" She sat at his desk, feeling his hand resting on her back. She just barely restrained herself from leaning into it.

"Here. This is the list of what I plan to play." He reached for the computer keyboard and mouse and showed her the list. "Take a look at it and see what you think."

Kitlin's attention went to the list, surprised to see the songs.

"You really do play the oldie-goldies, don't you?" She looked up at him, a pleased look on her face.

"I do." He stood, reaching for her hand, his eyes on the clock. "I need to get to the studio and get ready. You need to get back to the reception area. Ian said that they would be around and about for the day."

"That's what Streeter has said. He has hired security to be around when we're here. But what when we are not here? Would everyone be safe?"

"They'll make sure of it." Avery reached to hug her once more and then watched as she walked away.

Ian stood back where he could watch the couple, nodding to himself. Lydia, you were correct. They are a couple, even if they won't acknowledge it yet. Please, Lord, protect them and bring the investigation to a safe, early resolution.

Chapter 21

Stretching as he rose at the end of his show, Avery looked around. It had been good to be back. *Thank you, Lord, for understanding people that I work with. It has helped tremendously. Now to find Kitlin and see what she wants to do for the rest of the day. A meal at Mac's sounds good but I'm not sure that we should go there.*

Heading for the reception area, he could hear Ian's laugh and then Kitlin's voice protesting in a laughing manner as well. He stood where he could watch her, finding Micah at his shoulder, a grin on his face.

"What's going on?" Avery kept his voice low.

Micah began to laugh, knowing what Ian had been up to.

"He's offering to fly her somewhere to keep her safe until Frankie solves this. He's done that with most of the ladies who were in danger."

"He does, does he? And how much are you all working on this?" Avery gave a grin as he moved forward, wrapping Kitlin in a hug.

Kitlin gave a small scream, quickly covered by the laughter of the men with her. Streeter had appeared, knowing that the couple was getting ready to leave.

"All right, you two. Off you go. It's been a good day. Now, stay safe."

Avery walked his home late that night. He needed to retire, but his mind was too active to do just that. He worried about Kitlin, searching for his phone and sending off a text. He hesitated but shrugged as he added hearts to his message. He had no idea why he did that.

Kieren leaned against the kitchen counter, listening to Avery's soft footsteps. He sighed. Avery was in love and in danger but didn't know how to solve that mystery. Kieren had spent time with Jake that morning, Jake not working. They had wandered the town, particularly the downtown area, Jake looking for answers that weren't forthcoming. Frankie had been around, picking his brain as he stated it. None of them had any answers.

Avery appeared in front of him, an envelope in his hand. Kieren was puzzled as to when it had appeared. He had not seen anything earlier.

"Where did this come from, Kieren?" Avery was puzzled.

"I have no idea. I haven't seen it until now." He pushed away from the counter to stand beside him. "It has no name on it."

"No, it doesn't. It appears that we are now starting to get the stuff, as it's called. We had hoped to avoid it." Avery sighed, reaching for his phone. "Frankie? Are you still on call?"

"I am. What did you get?" Frankie reached to start his car. He had just walked away from another crime and had been taking time to make notes.

"An envelope. No name. No address." Avery turned it over. "It's not sealed."

"Don't open it. I'm on my way." Frankie was as good as his word, walking up to Avery's house in just a matter of minutes. He took the letter handed to him, his eyes on Avery and then Kieren. "You have no idea when it came?"

"No. I found it with the mail when I picked it out of the box late this evening. I hadn't looked there earlier." Avery leaned against the stove, his arms crossed across his chest, and his eyes on Frankie.

Frankie snapped on gloves and then studied the envelope. There was nothing on the outside to indicate what the contents would be. He pulled out the letter, unfolding it, and then reading it. His thoughts grew troubled. This was not a threat. And that was bizarre. In his experience, this never happened. These letters were always threats.

"This is strange, Avery. It is not a threat. Instead, it offers clues to what happened." Frankie looked up at a sound from Avery. "Avery?"

"The man who let us out and then left a map for us. Kitlin is positive that he was an angel."

Frankie stared at him before sharing a look with Kieren, who was nodding.

"Kieren? Those are your thoughts as well?"

"They are. Kitlin has talked with me. We were raised to believe that angels are sent from God and that we may never know who they are. This is entirely possible, based on what God has said in His word."

Avery was nodding.

"It is entirely possible, Frankie. I know of a lady who had an angel watching over her for years. Once she was safe and married, he disappeared and she never saw him again."

Frankie felt chills running up and down his spine and not from the cold weather outside.

"This puts a new twist to the case." He looked back down at the notes. "Do you know an Ethan Sweetman?"

"No, I don't recognize that name. Should I?" Avery reached to tilt Frankie's hand to read the note. "I would like a copy of that." His phone was out and he snapped a photo, before Frankie could say anything. "I need to show this to Kitlin." He yawned. "Sorry, guys. I need to crash. Morning comes early."

Frankie and Kieren watched him walk away, before they shared a look. They spoke for a few more minutes before Frankie gathered his evidence bags and walked away, puzzlement but also wonder in his thoughts. Was it possible? Was there a guardian angel involved?

Chapter 22

Late that week, Kitlin turned from the phone at work, troubled by the call that she had just ended. The caller, a man who was trying to disguise his voice, had been trying to find out information about herself and Avery, trying to portray himself as a fan of Avery's. Kitlin had not believed that for one minute. She rose, heading for Streeter.

"Streeter? I just had a strange call." She paused in his office doorway.

"What made it strange?" He sat back and watched her closely, seeing her upset.

"Whoever it was, he was fishing for information on Avery and also myself. He said he was a fan but I don't buy that."

"No, it's best not to. We don't have many calls like that. We'll let Frankie know and he can try and trace the number. Does that work for you?"

"It does. We are making a lot of work for him with no end in sight."

"No, you're not." Streeter's gaze moved behind her to see Avery appearing there. "Avery?"

"I heard. I don't like it, Streeter. Today's Friday. We're off until Monday. We'll try and stay safe, but that may be difficult."

Avery stood outside Kitlin's door, watching as she reached for the door. His hand stopped her, something warning him that there was danger inside. He grabbed her hand and walked her away from there, a puzzled look on her face.

"Avery? I need to go in my apartment." She struggled to release her hand.

"No, you don't. We need Frankie or Jake or someone to go through it." Avery searched for the officer who had just walked them to her door, waving him back. "Josh? I don't like the feeling that I got at Kitlin's apartment. Her parents are back home at their place. Can you go through it for us?"

Josh nodded, his eyes searching Kitlin's face, seeing the fear that she was trying hard to hide. He reached for her keys, pointing to his vehicle.

"Stand there by my car. John's on his way. He'll stay with you while I go through your home." He walked away, waving at the other officer who had just arrived.

John stood with the couple, not saying much. But then, words really weren't necessary. These two were in danger, although the culprits were not known at this point.

Josh walked back towards them, handing Kitlin back her keys. He looked past them, without saying anything. John nodded, heading back for his car, calling in help. Josh turned to Kitlin, not saying much.

"How bad is it, Josh?" Avery wrapped an arm around Kitlin, feeling her trembling with fear.

"Bad enough. We're going to be a while, Kitlin. We'll need the crime scene team to go through it.

Frankie is off today but Jake is working. He'll come and talk with you. For now? We need to get you two somewhere out of sight." Josh looked around as John walked back to him. "John?"

"I spoke with Caleb. He wants these two out of sight somewhere. I'm taking them to Avery's home for now. That may change." John pointed to his vehicle. "In there, you two. Now."

Avery nodded, heading that way, Kitlin's hand tight in his. He had had a bad feeling when he had heard about that phone call. He now wondered what its connection was to this. It was almost as if the caller had been trying to find out if they had both been still at the station. He said as much to John, who nodded. That was something that would be looked into.

Kitlin stared at the clock for a moment, then reached into the fridge. Avery was at the counter, making coffee for them, speaking quietly with John about the weather. She was afraid, she decided, and wanted this over. Christmas was coming and she wanted to celebrate it with her family and yes, Avery, this year without this hanging over their heads. Only it didn't seem that would happen.

Avery walked towards the door, the doorbell catching his attention. Frankie and Jake both stood there. He pointed to the kitchen, not saying anything. He could see the stern looks on their faces and sighed. Kitlin would not be going home that night.

Frankie took with thanks the plate of food handed him. He had been out and about that day, Deirdre away with her aunt, and he had not had a chance to grab his supper. He listened to the conversation around the table, hearing the underlying concern and fear that was present.

Avery rose, clearing the table and refilling the coffee mugs before he sat, his arm around Kitlin.

"Frankie? You're here? I thought that you were off today."

"I was, but Jake called me." Frankie drew in a deep breath. "Kitlin, we have gone through your apartment. It has been trashed to put it mildly. You won't be going back there for now. I spoke with the apartment building manager. We have agreed that your lease will stand but we can't have you putting the other tenants at risk. For now, we need to find somewhere to put you."

"And just where would that be? I need a place to live." Tears sparkled in her eyes for a moment.

"We understand that. Abe has offered a place for you, but we don't agree with that. Let me explain. Abe has a compound that houses his team members. He also has cabins that he offers for situations such as yours. However, he and his team need to be away for a few days on a security assignment. Therefore, we are looking for somewhere here in town."

"Kieren is staying here. Kitlin can as well. That shouldn't be a problem. I have the basement set up as a suite for whatever is needed. Kitlin can use that." Avery watched the conflicting emotions crossing her face.

Kitlin finally nodded, knowing that she had to stay somewhere and it might as well be where her brother was. At least then, she'd have family with her.

Chapter 23

Kitlin pulled the covers up over her ears that night, not quite sure that she was where she would be safe. She was also not sure how safe it was for her to be around Avery. She sighed, her thoughts troubled as she began to pray. Her eyes closed and she slept, but her sleep was restless. The dreams or nightmares raged all night, and she awoke tired and grumpy.

Kieren watched his sister closely, knowing just how tightly she was wound. He wanted to relieve that for her, but couldn't. This was something only she could do. He heard Avery moving around in his office and then turned to walk that way.

"Avery, what are your plans for today?"

"My plans? I need to get some groceries and then I was hoping to do some Christmas shopping. Why?"

"That's what I want to do. I am contributing to the household. I am living here." Kieren walked away, heading back for his sister.

Avery stood at his desk, staring at the computer, before he sat, pulling up a word processing program that he had been keeping notes on what they were going through. He read back through them, trying to find a common thread but just not finding it. He rose at last, heading for his jacket, reaching for Kitlin's hand.

Walking the downtown streets of his hometown, Avery nodded and greeted those he knew. He was uncomfortable out in the open, but he was refusing to hide anymore. Kitlin and he had talked, both in agreement with this. Kieren had simply listened, nodding. Aubrey and Aveleen had been vocal with their support, their spouses simply asking what they planned to do. They were on board with whatever their plan was.

Avery was making no secret of his interest in Kitlin. Not any more, he decided. She was the one who completed him, the one who he had been waiting for, the one who he would love ore and more each day. He would catch that look in her eyes, saying that she felt the same but neither one of them was ready to admit their feelings. That would come. They were just both afraid for the other.

Sitting at a table in Mac's cafe, Avery shrugged out of his jacket, letting it rest on the chair behind him. They had been joined by Micah and his wife, Kataleen, and Matt and his wife, Sarah. Laughter lit their faces, bringing needed joy and release to the couple going through this adventure.

"You two need to come out to the compound." Kat knew that they were planning a get-together for their friends and wanted Avery and Kitlin to attend. "There would be a lot of security there, you know."

Micah began to laugh harder at his wife's words.

"That there would be. Lots of it. We would welcome both of you. You've been there at one of our times before, Avery. Kitlin, you do need to come. And

Kieren, you too." He sobered for a moment. "Your parents are safe?"

"They are. Dad has had to go back to Ottawa for a week or so, just to finish up with his head office the final paperwork. Then, they plan to put their house up for sale. For some reason, they don't think Kitlin is leaving this town." He dodged the elbow that Kitlin directed his way.

"They are? That's good. Your father will be looking for something to do. We can find something. And you?" Matt had spoken up.

"I plan on opening my lawn care business here. It was suggested that I do something that would compliment Timothy's, only for low income people and single mothers or single fathers."

"We don't have something like that. Murphy's Adriel would be a good one to connect with. She works to help women and children who need legal aid. She used to work for the shelter until she left there." Matt shared a look with Micah. "Listen. Any word on your adventure?"

"Not a word. Yesterday someone called the station, on a fishing expedition. And then my apartment was broken into." Kitlin drew in a deep, shuddering breath. "I want this over, but it doesn't seem like it is going anywhere."

"It's not right at the moment. We did receive a letter from the person who we think is the one that freed us. We have no other information on that. Frankie said that given the lack of anything going on, they need to set it to a back burner for now. But they will still work it."

"And Emma and Jace are working it, as they can. They have been swamped with urgent searches and that is bothering Emma that she has to put yours to one side. She has asked one of her employees who lives out of town to work on it. Evan said that he was finding some information but was still waiting for more to come through." Micah didn't say anything more, but he shared a look with Avery who nodded.

"Now, what are we to do with the rest of the day?" Kieren laughed at the look on his sister's face. "It's December, Kitlin. We always do stuff in December."

"I know we do. Mom's not here, but we could bake. I have her cookie recipes saved to the cloud, so we could do that. Who wants to bake?" Kitlin grinned at the response, as all agreed that was exactly what they wanted to do.

Late that afternoon, Kitlin turned from cleaning the kitchen, the smell of baking still lingering in the air. She had enjoyed herself, finding the four from Abe's group a lot of fun, she thought. Kieren had been on a roll, teasing everyone, bringing a lightness to the air that was needed. Avery had stood back for a while, just watching before he joined in, stealing samples despite the threats launched at him from the ladies.

Avery simply came up behind Kitlin and wrapped her into his arms, his chin resting on her head, as she wiped out the sink. She stood for a moment before the cloth dropped and her hands found his.

———

"Have a good time today, sweetheart?" Avery's voice was soft, knowing what the answer would be. He had fallen more in love with her that day.

"I did. They are quite the people, you know. I have missed that. My friends have moved on, married, having a family, in different towns with work. I don't really have anyone close to talk with."

"You won't have that problem now, I can guarantee you that. Those two ladies? They are part of a wonderful group, who will just take you in. You can be friends with them all, but there will be some who will be closer to you. Aveleen has found that as had Finlee." He dropped a kiss on the top of her head, content just to hold her.

Chapter 24

Monday found Avery staring at the back door of the station, reading the note tacked there. It was not good, he thought, a hand outstretched for Kitlin's. It was a direct threat, he thought, finding Nathaniel pocketing his phone once more. Nathaniel pointed to the door, gloves on his hands before he opened it and ushered them in.

"Find what you need to do, Avery and Kitlin. I'll come and find you once the crime scene team is done." Nathaniel walked through the station, searching and not finding that someone had been able to get in. He nodded at the security guard walking back his way. "Did you see anyone on the feed?"

"Not a thing. There was a blip for a minute or so. I suspect that's when the note was left." The man was frustrated. "How did they do that?"

"Micah will be in contact with your office and search it out. I'm not sure, though, that we will find anything." Nathaniel turned back to face the office area. "This is where it gets worse for those two. We don't know who or why. It could be anyone."

"That's what we think. Avery has been good to all of us here. Streeter has used our company for years. He's always been fair with us. None of us want to see Avery or his lady hurt, at least not more than they have been." He walked away, to head outside to do his rounds.

———

Nathaniel stood in the reception area, searching. There seemed to be something off but he couldn't see anything that set off the warning sound in his head. He reached for the key and unlocked the door to the mail compartment, not finding anything. There was something, but he just couldn't put a finger on it.

Kitlin had been watching him before she moved past him, sitting at her desk, sticking her backpack under the desk. She reached for the phone, intent on retrieving the voice messages. The last one had her freezing, fear on her face. Nathaniel had been watching her intently and reached for the phone, keying the message back to the beginning. He saved it and then hung up the phone. Crouching down beside Kitlin, Nathaniel's hand rested on her arm.

"Kitlin? Is this the first one like this that has come into the office?" He waited patiently for her to answer.

Kitlin finally nodded, open fear on her face. Her voice shook when she finally responded to him.

"It is. A little brutal, I would say. Why leave a message like that here?"

"Because they can't reach you any other way. They wouldn't have your cell number or Avery's for that matter. I know that his is an unlisted number and has been for years." Nathaniel rose, pacing. "I need to talk to Frankie or Jake about this. Streeter is on his way in."

"Maybe I should just quit work and move away." She was sober as she spoke, blinking back tears. She had grown to love Riverville, the shops, and the people. Moving away would mean moving away from Avery, and that she just wasn't prepared to do. Not yet. Maybe not ever.

"That never works. They would find you and bring you back. They have connected you and Avery, likely because you were here when they abducted him in the first place. Has anything else happened that you just brushed off?" Nathaniel was intent on her answers, hearing the sounds of Avery signing in on air through the station system.

"I don't know. I don't know what to look for. But I just have this feeling of doom, of something about to happen. It's like I'm standing on the brink of a falls, ready to go over, and just can't stop what is going to happen." She blinked for a moment, her attention on Nathaniel. "I know that I am not sleeping, too worried to do that. I worry about Avery being hurt or disappearing forever from his family. And I worry about Kieren getting caught in the middle of all this. I don't want my big brother hurt."

"We understand that, Kitlin. We don't want that to happen either. Let me follow up with Frankie or Jake. They were on their way. I know it's difficult to work under these circumstances, especially in a new position, but our promise to you is that we will do the best we can to keep you both safe." Nathaniel walked away, leaving Kitlin to turn to her desk, reaching for the phone as it rang.

Frankie walked through the station, listening to Avery's commentary on his songs. He had done that many times before, but this time? There was an undercurrent in his voice that paused Frankie's forward walk. *He's scared*, Frankie thought. *He's scared and trying hard to hide it. Lord, please protect these two. Keep them safe. Help us to find the culprits before they are harmed in any other way.*

Kitlin looked around from the mail that she was sorting, not surprised to find Frankie there. It was now mid-afternoon. She had been worried and scared all day, her fear growing with each beat of her heart. This is not how she had planned her day. Not at all. Only someone seemed to be directly how she made it through the time. That angered her. And with Kitlin, anger drove her to act.

"Frankie? What can you tell me?"

"Not a lot. But can I listen to that voice mail?" Frankie sat in her chair, watching as she pulled up the message for him. He listened to it, before he pulled out his phone and recorded it. There was something there in the background, a sound that was familiar but he wasn't quite sure what it was. "As Nathaniel said, a little brutal. Now, when is Avery done?"

Kitlin squinted at the clock.

"In about five minutes." She reached for her mug, heading for the kitchen, ready to wash it and put it away. Her hand froze as she reached to place the mug in the cupboard, dropping it instead to the counter. It shattered to pieces even as she backed away, hands covering her mouth to still her scream. Nathaniel was there in seconds, a hand to his weapon, searching for what had caused the alarm.

Pointing to the cupboard, Kitlin's finger was shaking. Fear rose within her, darkening her vision.

———

120

She screamed as she felt arms around her, Avery at her side almost as soon as Nathaniel was. Streeter stood in the doorway, Frankie pushing by him, heading for the cupboard. The men stared at the image posted in there, before Frankie and Nathaniel were out of the room, searching for whoever it was that had placed the picture there.

———

Chapter 25

Avery leaned against the wall outside of the kitchen, his arms still around Kitlin. She had finally stopped shaking, but he could see the stark fear on her face. Somehow, someone had made it into the station and left that graphic photo. He could not unsee it. A tombstone? Who does that, he wondered? And just what did it say? He had not been allowed close enough to see it.

Frankie turned from speaking with Nathaniel. They just couldn't determine how someone had made it into the station building. There were no unusual blips on the feed. That had already been determined. That left someone who worked here. And Streeter was adamant that he trusted all of his employees. And no stranger had been around that day.

Walking to the back door, Frankie cracked it open, studying the lock. He pointed to something. Nathaniel drew a deep breath. Someone had tampered with the lock. And did that really mean one of the station staff was responsible?

"What do we do with these two, Frankie?" Nathaniel had already been in touch with Abe, who was on his way in from the compound. "Abe's on his way in."

"We can't lock them away. They won't do that. Kitlin is ready to run. And Avery will go right after her. They want to continue to live their lives." Frankie eyed the two, finding them watching him in return. "How close are they?"

"I have no idea. They're not saying. We're not picking up that they're a couple. Not like we were."

"No, they're not a couple. They're close friends, at least I think they are." Frankie sighed, hearing his phone chime. He pulled it out, walking away to talk with Caleb. "Caleb?"

"Frankie, talk to me. What happened?" Caleb sat behind his desk, eyeing the piles of paperwork that he should be working on but they could wait, at least for now

"Someone has gained access to the station. A graphic photo of a tombstone was in the kitchen cabinet. We can't figure out how they made it in and out. The back door seems to have been tampered with but we're not seeing anything on the security feed."

"That's strange. Have Micah run it for you. He's been working with the company." Caleb thought through what was going on. He was becoming increasingly worried about his wife's cousin and his lady. "We did a check on the company, did we not?"

"We did. But I've asked Emma or Jace to run the company and their employees. Other than the station staff, they're the only ones who have been around the back door. I need to talk with Streeter. We may have to pull them off the security for now, until we determine exactly who is responsible for this."

"I talked with Streeter about that. He has agreed to that. I would suggest we talk with Richard or Don and see if they can step in to help with security for those two. This is when it's going to get worse. We're coming up to the holidays and I would like to see this resolved by then."

"Unfortunately, I don't think it will be. Listen. I have to head over to the other side of town. Another murder there. What is it lately? We just have so many cases." Frankie walked towards his car, the key fob in his hand to unlock the doors.

"I know. We've been saying that for a while. It's like whoever it is wants to spread our resources thin." Caleb grew quiet. "Frankie, when you're done there, come and find me. Bring Jake with you. I want to pull you two off most of your cases that we can. I think we're on the right track with this. Someone is setting us up for something. What other festivals and events do we have that are upcoming that would draw a lot of tourists into town? I would hate to see a repeat of Doug and Darcy."

Frankie grew quiet, even as his vehicle moved through the town. Caleb was correct, he thought. They had the big parade upcoming in a couple of weeks as well as the tree lighting ceremony that weekend. Both events drew people into their town. And then there was that charity concert upcoming. Nathaniel's wife, Elizabeth, was part of it as a concert pianist. She was reluctant to take part but had agreed as the proceeds went to the shelters and charities in town.

"I hear you, Caleb. I think that you are correct. Let me get through this and then I'll come and find you. We may need to bring in Doug. Have we talked to Darcy about doing a profile on this case?"

———

"She's ahead of you, Frankie. I have that on my desk. She dropped in off about an hour ago."

"Good.   I'll head in there shortly.   In the meantime, what do we do with Avery and Kitlin?" Frankie parked at the new crime scene, his eyes on the yellow tape surrounding the area.

"That I don't have an answer for." Caleb rose, walking through the department, not quite sure what he needed to do. Frankie is right, he thought.

Avery turned from closing his house door, Kieren standing in the living room doorway. Kitlin had disappeared downstairs without saying a word to her brother. He had watched her walk away and then turned to Avery.

"Avery? What happened?"

"Someone left a brutal voice mail today. Yes, Frankie has it. And then this afternoon, Kitlin found a photo of a tombstone or gravestone or whatever you want to call it in the kitchen cupboard at work." Avery's hands ran through his hair. "We don't get it. We don't know how that happened."

"And you're sure about all the people who work at the station?" Kieren knew that he was asking the obvious but still had to.

"We are.   At least, I think we are.   It's the security company that I'm not sure of. Nathaniel said Micah would take over the feed for now and see what he could find." Avery looked up, devastation on his face. He didn't see the photos and pictures on the wall of the living room. He just didn't see anything other

———

125

than the look on Kitlin's face when he found her. "We need to stop this. Only I have no idea how to. And we don't know who is behind it all."

Chapter 26

Kitlin walked through the downtown area the next afternoon. She had slipped away from her security detail, not by chance but by choice. She needed some alone time. Avery had watched her walk away and sighed. *She's putting herself out there, isn't she?* He turned and walked in the opposite direction, heading for his home. It was a warmer day, the snow that had fallen already melting. He paused at the centre of town, his eyes on the large evergreen tree that was set to be lit the next night. It was the official start of the Christmas season in Riverville. His head turned as he felt a presence beside him. Dave Allison stood on his one side, Doug Foster on the other.

"Avery? Where's your security?" Doug looked around, trying to find them.

"I sent them home. It's never going to be resolved if we're kept under wraps. Kitlin is moving home this weekend. She needs that. Kieren is heading back to his hometown, getting his business closed, and packing his house. He's sold it and has found property here that works to house both himself and his business." Avery waited for the condemnation that he figured he would hear.

"About what we expected you to do." Dave nodded in agreement. "It's time you two took back your life. And you can't date her if you're with security all the time. That just doesn't work."

"No, it doesn't. We both hate being under the microscope, as must as we know that is that is needed." Avery sighed. "I've talked to just about everyone who I can talk to. They all same the same thing. That they all wanted to run and be free of whatever security that they were under."

"We all did." Dave agreed with his sentiments. "Doug was different. Being an officer, it was difficult for him to escape that. Darcy tried, I know, but didn't get very far."

Doug nodded.

"It was different for us. We have been involved with others. One thing I have learned? That each couple may face what seems to be the same threat, but it is individual to them. The reasons why are part of it. The other part is who is after them. And I don't think that we have come up with that for you two."

Avery agreed. He turned thoughtful eyes to Doug.

"Doug, are you both free tonight? And your wives? Can we get together? I am sure Kitlin would like to hear your thoughts." He turned as he felt a hand on his back.

Kitlin stood there. Her eyes were watchful, not sure if she should have joined them. She felt an arm wrapped around herself and was drawn closer to Avery.

"Avery? Making plans for me?" Her tone was slightly teasing, slightly questioning.

"I was. I was coming to find you. Doug and Dave are free tonight. I think that we need to meet with them. You need to hear their stories." He grinned as she snorted, causing the other two men to try and hide their grins.

"Them too? I thought I had heard all of them."

"No, I don't think you have. We have had many friends go through things. Let's head home, then, sweetheart. Doug? Dave?"

"We'll be there. Rylee will bring dessert." Dave waved as he walked away, leaving Kitlin staring after him, her mouth open.

"It's okay, Kitlin." Doug grinned as her frown turned towards him. "Rylee has the Irish bake shop. She's always giving her friends treats."

That evening, Darcy, Doug's wife, watched Kitlin closely. She was a retired forensics psychologist and while she no longer practiced that, she still was available for friends to talk with. She knew that Kitlin was hiding something but that she was also ready to run.

"Kitlin?" Darcy's voice caused Kitlin to turn towards her, oven mitts still on her hands. "Are you okay?"

Kitlin stopped moving, her eyes on the oven, before she pulled out the casserole that she had prepared and then set it on top of the stove. She drew off the mitts, all the while thinking through what she had been asked.

Kitlin turned back to Darcy, finally shaking her head.

"No, I don't think that I am. I am puzzled about how I got involved in this. Who is responsible for this. Why Avery was targeted. We don't have any answers. We can't describe or identify the men responsible for kidnapping us. How do I go on?"

Darcy nodded, knowing that Doug and Dave were speaking with Avery, asking him the same questions. Rylee turned from where she had been setting the table, her eyes thoughtful as well.

"You are describing exactly how you feel. You've been dropped into a new town, new work, new friends, and then into a situation where you had no control. You were kept captive for a number of days, in not so nice conditions. You are worried about your brother and your parents as well. You don't know if the culprit will go after them." Darcy paused, a thought coming to her. "Did you listen to this radio station before you moved here?"

Kitlin stared at her, her eyes widening at the question.

"No, I didn't. I really didn't listen to any music. This job came up and I applied, not really expecting to be hired. I was. Now, how do we solve this? What can you suggest?"

Darcy nodded, her thoughts racing.

"How be we eat, and then we can discuss this? I did a profile that I passed on to Frankie. I will let you have a copy as well. I don't think that there is just one person involved. There never usually is."

Rylee was nodding, her arm around Kitlin.

"I agree. I think that you will find there is more than one involved. And it will likely be directed at Avery. Possibly Streeter. You know, Darcy, with what Aveleen and Aubrey went through, it just didn't seem as if it had been totally resolved. There has always been something hanging."

The three women looked up as they heard a strangled sound. Avery stood there, devastation on his face, knowing that the ladies were right. Something had seen to be unfinished.

Chapter 27

Dave and Doug exchanged a glance as they rose from the table. This was where it became difficult, they knew, trying to come to an understanding of what was going on. Avery had headed for the door, the doorbell ringing as he had risen as well.

Abe and Emma stood in the doorway, watching the five in the kitchen. Emma handed Abe the files that she was holding and headed for Kitlin, simply hugging the lady. She could feel the suppressed sobs that shook Kitlin's body for a moment before she stepped back, her head nodding at Emma. Emma took in her looks, seeing the stress and strain on her face.

"Kitlin? We need to talk. Can we sit in the living room?" Her arm around her, Emma drew her into that room.

Avery reached for Kitlin's hand, drawing her to a seat on the couch, his arm around her. He glanced around at his friends, finding their eyes all on him before he spoke.

"Abe? We need to pray. That is the only thing that will get us through this. I feel like I have been walking in a desert for weeks now, a pauper in things related to my faith. I know that's not true."

"Not it's not true, but it is how we feel." Abe knew from experience that feeling, having been separated from Emma for ten years through the machinations of a cruel man. "I agree that we need to

132

pray and pray fervently. This is when it gets tough and rough. And we need to be steadfast in keeping you two upheld in our prayers.”

Thirty minutes later, their heads raised, the presence of God in the room.

“Okay, people. This is what I’ve found.” Emma reached for the folders and opened the top one. “It doesn’t directly involve the radio station. It is being painted as that. Streeter is not the actual target. You are for some reason, Avery. I am still working on the reason why, but that is not clear at the moment. But we have some ideas that we are running. I am hoping to have more answers tomorrow.

“For now, let’s concentrate on what we do know. As I said, it is directed at you, Avery. And we know there are at least two people involved. The names are not clear as yet. We’re working through a number of aliases and numbered companies. Anything that we confirm is being passed on to Frankie for him to investigate and confirm the information. We have determined that there is both a man and woman involved. It appears that they are well established in town but are in hiding. From you, we do know that there are at least two men who work for them. The house where you were kept? We have tracked it down and Frankie is aware of that. We can’t say much more than that right now.”

Kitlin was frustrated, and it showed on her face.

“What can you tell us?”

“What can we tell you?” Abe sat forward, his elbows on his knees. “That this is where it becomes very dangerous for you both. They are tracking you. We have found evidence of that. They know where you work, where you live, and who your friends are."

"We realize that. They also know who our families are and where they live. How do we protect everyone? Or is that even possible?" Avery was thinking through the ramifications of what could happen.

"They know that, for sure." Doug took over the conversation. "We've been brainstorming on what you can do."

"And what would you suggest?" Kitlin stared at him, a mutinous look on her face.

Doug grinned at her, motioning to Darcy.

Darcy began to speak, her eyes not wavering from the couple in front of her.

"These people? They will up what they are doing, trying to catch either one of you on your own. Kitlin, they will go after you to get to Avery. Avery, you know how it works. They will threaten Kitlin to get to you. They will threaten your family. The longer and harder we make it for them to get to you, the more this will escalate.

"The two are related. They are an older couple, likely married, or brother and sister. They are professionals. The feeling that I am getting is that they are after something that they think you have. What that is? I don't have a sense of that yet. But you must be very careful from now on. They will not hesitate to kill one of you or anyone else who gets in their way."

Kitlin whitened at that. That was her fear, that whoever it was would kill someone in their families. Only how did they prevent that? She asked that, her gaze shifting between the four men.

Abe nodded, knowing that Kitlin had gone to the very heart of the matter.

"That we are working on. My team will continue their escort and security presence as they can. There are officers who are also volunteering on their off time. I have two friends with security teams who will be coming on board as well. Our sense is that this will all blow up in the next two to three weeks."

Doug nodded, having that same thought.

"They seem to be running out of time. Word reaching us from the street is that this has to be resolved soon. The cargo that you saw? We have tracked down the van, and our friends on the street are following it and watching the driver. If he tries anything at all, they will step in. They have all promised to watch for you whenever you are out and about. And they will. First for your sakes. Then for Frankie. He was on the streets for years and they do everything that they can to help him, just because of how he helped so many of them."

Chapter 28

The next afternoon, Avery wandered the downtown area once more, this time with Kitlin's hand tight in his. Aubrey and Finlee were with them, with promises from Aveleen and Logan to meet up with them for a meal. Laughter flushed Kitlin's face for the moment, her thoughts not on the danger that they were facing.

Aubrey studied his brother, seeing a freedom in him that he had not seen in years. The family had known that Avery had been struggling. Only, they could not get him to speak about it. He would just shrug and walk away, leaving them standing and staring after him. He resolved at that point to find time to thank Kitlin for what she was doing for his brother.

Finlee wrapped her arm around Kitlin, pulling her into a store, seeking for a gift for her

"In here, Kitlin. They have all sorts of neat trinkets and doodads, as Dad calls. Now, what can we find for you?"

"For me?" Kitlin stared around the story, mesmerized by the selection. "I don't need anything."

"But you see, you do. You need something tangible to remind you that God loves you and has your best in mind. No matter what we face, He is there in the midst of it. He calms the storms within and without. He provides protection for us. Sometimes, He allows us to go through things that we would rather not, but at no time does He ever abandon us. There are times when we need something that we can touch just to remind us of that."

Kitlin finally nodded, moving through the store, standing at last in front of a small ornament of a mother bird sheltering a baby, the baby peeking out from under a wing.

"This, Finlee. This." Kitlin picked it up, only to have Finlee take it from her. "Finlee?"

"It's my gift to you. I suspect that you will be part of our family at some point. Avery is more relaxed and more at peace than I have seen him. Aubrey says he is more like he was years ago. And that is because of you. I can tell that he is falling in love with you. I see it in his eyes. And I suspect that you are falling in love with him." Her hand up, Finlee stopped Kitlin from speaking. "That is a discussion that you two need to have. I pray that you have it soon." She was away and back in short order, handing Kitlin the small gift bag. "Now, let's find our fellows."

Avery wrapped an arm around Kitlin, snugging her tight to him as they watched the lights begin to flicker on the tree. He wished that she would stay with him forever. Only he was afraid to ask, not wanting to hear that she was leaving town. He sometimes caught her watching him, a look in her eyes that said he was special.

Aveleen watched her brother and then looked around, feeling uncomfortable. They were being watched, that much she knew. Only she could not see anyone who stood out. Logan shared a look with her and then looked around as well. They were planning on heading to his brother's place the next day, just for a day's visit, and he worried about his brother-in-law.

"Avery? Is it always like this?" Kitlin's face was alight with wonder. "This is amazing!"

"It is. They really do a lot to celebrate Christmas here. There is a town that we need to visit at some time. It really is called Mistletoe. Christmas is a really big time for them. I've been there at that time of year." He paused for a moment, reliving that day. "We'll go there one year, sweetheart."

Kitlin stared up at him, knowing that he was speaking from his heart. He looked down at her then, his heart in his eyes. She sighed, her head going against his arm. This was something that they really needed to discuss. Only that would not happen that night.

Walking back through the crowd, Avery and Kitlin became separated from the other two couples. Afterwards, they were not sure how that happened. However it was, it left them vulnerable. Frankie and Deirdre were just behind them, and Frankie could never quite explain what happened.

A hand reached out and grasped Kitlin's arm, pulling her away from Avery and towards an alleyway. Avery gave a shout and headed after her, not realizing that Frankie was running towards him, shouldering his way through the crowds. Doug had been standing there, on duty that night and followed, his second-in-command heading after him.

———

Kitlin struggled to free herself, her hand hitting and slapping at the man who held her arm. He simply wrapped his arms around her, trapping hers at her side and picked her up. He almost ran from the area, not hearing the pounding footsteps that followed him. Kitlin still struggled to free herself, her head twisting and hitting back at him.

Then, it happened. In her struggles, she had been kicking at him. Her leg tangled with his and tripped him. He fell forward, trapping her underneath him. He didn't move for a moment and then shoved himself upright. He stared down at Kitlin, not quite believing what had happened. He stooped, intent on picking her up and running with her. Hands on his arms stopped him and dragged him away from her.

Avery was on his knees, an almost sob in his voice as he called for Kitlin. She lay still, unmoving at his call. Dave was there, coming from the other direction. Doug had reached out to him when he saw Kitlin fall before calling for help. He assessed her, turning to speak to the paramedics who had appeared. They nodded, one running to the rig for a backboard.

Standing with Doug's arm around his shoulder, Avery searched the area, seeing Frankie shoving the abductor away from them. He frowned at the man.

"That's one of them, Doug. Not the one who was the driver. The other one. Can we catch the head ones now?"

"I doubt it, but we can charge him with both abductions. That one and tonight. He'll also face assault charges." Doug would not vocalize his thoughts. They were too troubled for Kitlin. He prayed for her, watching as she was shifted to the backboard and then the stretcher. He held Avery back from following her.

"Not yet, Avery. Not yet. Kieren is here somewhere, isn't he?"

"He is. So are her parents." Avery's eyes slid shut as his head tilted up. "I thought that we would be safe. We weren't. When will we be?" He dropped his head, struggling with his emotions. *Please, Lord? Protect my lady. Don't let her be hurt badly. And let us find the ones responsible and soon.* He turned then and walked away, following the paramedics, to stand on the sidewalk, lost and uncertain as to what he should be doing. Aubrey approached him, as did Logan. They stood shoulder to shoulder, brothers united in fear and prayer.

Chapter 29

Avery paced the waiting room at the local hospital, his eyes on the door to the examination rooms. He knew that Kieren was around, he had spoken with him. Kieren had been shocked when Avery told him what had happened. Both men had bitten back words that they would not utter. Esther had simply wrapped Avery in a hug and prayed for him, Paul's arms around the two of them. He knew that his mom and dad were around, just for support for himself but also for Kitlin's people.

Caleb watched him before moving in. Hannah was around, he knew, somewhere with her cousins. That was a given. It was what she did. His hand laid on Avery's shoulder, stopping him in his tracks.

"Caleb? You're here. I thought Frankie was the one who was investigating this." Avery turned, worry on his face.

"He is, Avery. I'm here as family to support you." He drew Avery to one side, handing over a cup of coffee. "Hannah is with the families."

"Thank you. Now, what can we do? I want this over." Avery was growing angry, something that he very seldom did.

"We know, Avery. We know. Frankie is working on it tonight. Deirdre is here somewhere. She has called in Eddie and Ben. They'll be around at some point. They know their town. They still have resources and contacts that the others don't."

"I know. I just wish this hadn't happen. Kitlin was so happy tonight. She was just glowing." Avery turned to watch the door, sipping absentmindedly at the coffee. "Caleb, why?"

"Why? To get to you, more than likely. We need to sit down with you once more. We need to figure this out. Who do you know that wants to harm you? Did you see something that you shouldn't have? Meet someone that you shouldn't have?"

Avery nodded at Caleb's questions. They were the questions that he was asking himself, without any answers. He watched at Paul and Esther moved towards the doors, following the nurse who emerged to find them. Kieren followed rapidly from where he had been standing with Logan and Aubrey. Avery wanted to be there, but not being family meant that he couldn't.

Caleb watched with compassion as Avery walked away, dropping his coffee cup into the garbage. He was headed for somewhere, only he had no idea where he wanted to be other than where Kitlin was.

Esther reached to touch her daughter's hair, not liking it that Kitlin was not awake. They were still running tests, the nurse said, but the doctor felt that her parents needed to be with her. They would be asked to leave when they needed to.

Paul's heart was troubled even as it was raised in petition for his daughter. This was not what they had planned for the night. He had been told that her abductor was in custody but wasn't talking. That didn't sit well with him. Paul wanted to face him, to ask him why, but he would not get that chance.

Late that night, Kieren paced his sister's hospital room. He had refused to leave, just staring at the nurse. Her parents had reluctantly left, heading for her apartment to get some rest. They both knew that they would not be sleeping, instead spending the night in intercessory prayer. Kieren turned as he heard the door swish open. He figured it would be a nurse of even Frankie or Jake. Instead, Avery stood there.

"Kieren? Has she awakened?" Avery stopped at the side of the bed, watching as Kitlin slept. At least, he hoped that it was sleep.

"Not yet. They're not sure when she will. Apparently, her head hit hard and she has a concussion. She also had torn tendons in her shoulder." Kieren was saddened at the hurt that his sister had suffered.

"She does? I don't like that." Avery looked around, not realizing that there were tears on his face. "I couldn't stop him. It just happened so quickly."

"We understand that, Avery. No one blames you. We blame whoever it is that is behind this." Kieren slumped into a chair, his eyes on his sister. "She won't either."

"I know that. I just wish it was different." Avery rested his hand on Kitlin's, finding hers moving under his. "She's restless."

"She is. Pain is doing that to her." Kieren watched Avery closely. "What actually happened, Avery? I wasn't close enough to see."

———

"Someone just grabbed her and started to run. We think that she struggled, their legs tangled, and he fell on top of her." Avery had to quell his distress, and that was difficult to do. "I couldn't stop that from happening. I'm sorry."

"We get that, Avery. As I said, no one blames you. Has Frankie talked to you?"

"Frankie? No, he hasn't." Avery looked around, finding another chair to draw up to the bed. "You're not leaving."

"No, I'm not. There are officers around here for tonight, but I'm staying." Kieren was adamant on that. The physician had finally agreed, knowing that Kitlin needed him if she suddenly awakened and was on her own.

"I'm staying as well." Avery expected an argument. "I talked with Streeter. He wants Kitlin not to come in for now. We'll manage. He'll man the phones as he can, and his wife, Becky, will come in. She's done that before."

"She has? That's a relief. Kiltin wouldn't be working for a while."

"No, she won't. I hate that she was hurt. I am trying to determine who it is. Friends were around last night and we worked on it. Only we can't come to any conclusion as to who it is."

Kieren nodded, his thoughts troubling.

"What if it isn't you?" Avery turned to Kieren at that, understanding on his face at what the other man was asking. "What if it someone else and they blame you?"

"We have come to that conclusion. I need to speak with Frankie about that. Abe is bringing in other security teams to help. He is adamant on that."

"And you need it. I'm back in town now, but Kitlin will not want someone with her all the time. She'll begin to protest that as soon as she's out of here." Kieren frowned as Avery shook his head. "Avery?"

"Kitlin agreed to that. She's not happy, but she understands. After last night, it's a given that we need someone with her. Whoever it is? As Doug said, they'll go after Kitlin to get to me. I just wish I knew why." Avery's grief and fear rose to the surface and he fought to drive it back down. *Lord, please? Solve this and soon.*

Chapter 30

Kitlin shifted on the hospital bed, frowning at Frankie as he stood at the end, his notepad resting on the bedside table. She couldn't remember what happened.

"I have no idea what you're talking about, Frankie. When was this?"

"Last night. You were abducted again, pulled away from Avery, and then hurt. We think you tripped somehow and your abductor landed on you. Do you remember anything at all?" Frankie was pushing and they both knew it.

"No." Her eyes closed, the headache worsening with her stress. "I don't, Frankie. Please leave?"

Frankie tucked away his notepad and pen, his eyes thoughtful. She was not helping, he thought. And Saul, the man whom they had captured, wasn't speaking either. He either didn't know a lot or he was afraid of his boss. And experience told him that she wouldn't remember, at least not yet, if she ever did.

Kieren and Avery walked towards him as he stood outside her room.

"Frankie?" Kieren's eyes shot between Frankie and the open door. "Kitlin?"

"It's okay. She's sleeping again. Call me if she does remember anything." Frankie walked away,

———

leaving the other two men staring at one another and then the open door.

Esther and Paul had approached at that point. Their questioning looks drew a response from Kieren, who simply hugged his mother.

"Frankie was around, yes. But Kitlin is sleeping again." Kieren pointed to his father. "Dad, what are your thoughts?"

"My thoughts? That someone is not after Kitlin or even Avery." His hand went up as Avery's mouth opened. "Let's go into Kitlin's room. I have cleared with the hospital staff that she can have more than two visitors. We also have a security team moving in to provide security while we are here." He watched as his wife, his son, and the man who he suspected had his daughter's heart walked into the room. He pulled the door closed before he turned to the man standing nearby. "Richard?"

"Yes, Paul. My team is here. As we discussed, I have two men and two ladies on my team. We are available for the next week." Richard paused at that point, thinking through the process of keeping Kitlin and Avery safe. "I know Avery from town. He'll fight us at some point. And so will Kitlin."

"What are your thoughts on this? I've spoken with Frankie and Caleb. Neither one is saying much."

Richard rubbed at his neck, watching as his team members, Stephen and Silver, approached, taking up their positions in the waiting room and at the door. He had been approached by Abe, asking him for help. He didn't have a lot of information, but what he had been given concerned him.

"My thoughts? They're troubled at the moment. I don't think these two are free of whatever or whoever it is. They're just going into the worst part right now. I understand that there is not a lot of information as to it is the police are willing to release. I've spoken with Frankie. He has told me what he can. But they can't and won't compromise the investigation. And I understand and expect that.

"As to where we go from here? That I am not sure. Those two won't want to stay under guard for long. And we can't force them. It's concerning, I know. What I can tell you is that we will do the best that we can to protect them and keep them as safe as we can. Kitlin won't be working for a while. Avery will be, and I have spoken with Streeter. He is bringing in more security for now. All the staff are in agreement with that, he tells me. Avery is well thought of by his co-workers. So is Kitlin, even though she has not been there that long."

"That's good to hear. Thank you, Richard. Come on in and introduce yourself to the others." Paul entered the room, followed by Richard, to find his daughter sitting upright, anger on her face. "Kitlin?"

Kitlin struggled with her headache, not quite clear as to why she was where she was.

"Dad? Can we leave? I need to leave here. I'm not safe." Kitlin struggled with her tears, stress driving that.

"We can, Kitlin. But not today. They want to observe you for another day. And we need to talk about when you do go home. You will have someone with you that is in security at all times." His hand went up at her protest. "That is not an option, love. Not any more. You were abducted last night from the midst of a crowd. That shows their desperation at taking you. This is Richard. He has a team that will be with you from now on. At least for the next few weeks. Live with it. If you don't, you might not." Paul's expression was filled with compassion even as he spoke sternly with his daughter. It was how he knew that she needed to be addressed.

Kitlin slumped back on the upraised head of the bed, looking up at the ceiling. She knew her father was correct. Only that was not how she wanted to live. Only, if she didn't, she might not live.

Avery watched her closely before his eyes shifted to Richard, who in turn was watching him. Richard nodded. Avery sighed, knowing that they would be speaking. *Lord, I don't get it. What is going on? Who is the one behind all this? All I know is that my lady is troubled and hurt and I can't help her. Lord, You have promised to protect us, to draw us into the shelter of Your wings and find rest and relief. Thank you, Lord, that You are here with us. Drive us back to Your Word, to find what we need to keep us going.*

Richard nodded towards the door and moved that way, Avery following him.

"Richard?"

"Avery? What's going on? I don't think that you're the real target. Someone is using you to get to someone else. Only we don't have a handle on who that is."

"I know, Richard." Avery nodded to Stephen and Silver. "That's what we've begun to expect. Now, where do we go? I can't quit my job. Kitlin will want to be there as soon as she can, even working one handed."

"We know that, Avery, and we're working with Streeter on that. I understand that Micah and Joseph are revamping the security system and have pulled the company that had it. There are some red flags being raised now about them."

"There are? It thought they were a safe company to use."

"So did everyone else. Streeter is upset, to say the least."

Chapter 31

Avery walked through his house late the next night. He was due at work the next morning and needed to sleep. Only, he could not get his mind to understand that. He finally sat at his desk, a low light on, and pulled up his word processing program. Making notes, Avery sat back, surprise on his face. He had a good idea who it was now and knowing that he knew why. He would have to speak with his father. Only that would have to wait until he finished work the next day. Instead, he sent off an email to Michael, telling him what he had discovered and could he confirm the findings.

Michael had still been up, not able to sleep. Worry about his son had prevented him from relaxing. He read Avery's email and frowned. *Avery, what have you done? This person is so high in the town, I don't know if we can even prove anything. But we will do our best.* Michael sent the information on to Emma, knowing that she had likely already found that person. He reached for his phone, grimacing as he saw the time.

"Avery? You're not in bed, son. You need to sleep." Michael's voice held concern.

"I know, Dad. I just can't get to sleep. This is weighing too much on my mind. I hate that I'm being used. I hate that Kitlin has been hurt because of it." He swallowed hard, tears clogging his throat for a moment.

Michael prayed for his son, his audible words calming Avery.

"I know, son. I have your email. I've asked Emma to look into it more. Now, what can I do for you? You have our prayers. But what else can we do?"

"I don't know, Dad. I really don't know."

"It's okay, son, not to know. God knows. He's there with you, even when you don't feel Him. Your emotions are not trustworthy at this point. They are in such turmoil."

"I know, Dad. But what are your feelings on that name?" Avery reached for a pen and paper.

"Him? Yes, I could see him doing something like that. He's older than your Mom and me. I was in school with a brother of his. I never trusted the brother. There were always rumours about him, even back then. The name? There have been rumours over the years as to how he made his money. I have spoken with Caleb over the years, but neither one of us had the information that we needed to even have him investigated. His wife? She is not from our town. And there is speculation that they never married, were just living together, even though she calls herself his wife."

"I've heard that. Streeter has mentioned him at times. I thought that it was just talk."

"I would suspect not. Now, have you had any more packages or messages?"

"No, I haven't. That scares me, Dad. That means they are that close to us. I don't want to disappear again and be locked up somewhere. Only, that is a possibility that I have been forced to face.”

“It is, son. Our prayer is that as well, that you stay safe. Unfortunately, it not likes means that you will. This man’s brother would not hesitate to do anything for him, even to killing someone.” Michael stopped for a moment, his emotions overcoming him. When he could speak again, he changed topics. “Your mom and I are praying for you and your lady. We won’t pry as to your feelings for her. That is a discussion that you need to have with her first. But know this, son. If she is the lady who is God’s help-meet for you, you will know it.”

Avery nodded, even though his father could not see him.

“Thank you, Dad. That means a lot to me.”

Avery set his phone aside, a frown on his face. He rose and paced to the front door, cracking it open and peeking out. There was a package there. He sighed. This is not what he needed, not at this time of night. He returned to his office, reaching for his phone.

Jake, who was on duty that night, approached him.

“How did you know, Avery?”

Avery shrugged, not quite sure how to respond.

“I was speaking with Dad and mentioned that we hadn’t been getting those things. He said it was likely because they were so close to us. Now this.” He pointed at the package that the crime scene tech was working on. “What’s in it?”

———

"A note and a stuffed animal. We're working through what is in there. What else have you been up to?"

Avery sighed, pointing back towards the office.

"In there. I have a name. Dad knows the man and doesn't have a lot of good to say about him or his brother." He simply handed Jake a slip of paper.

Jake stared at it, knowing that this was the man that they suspected but had not been about to prove anything again. No matter how much that they had tried. And they had been trying for years to do that.

"How did you come up with him?"

Avery shrugged, not quite sure how he had.

"I just started listing names of those who were really prominent in town and went from there. He was one that made every list that I could come up with. Dad also said that his wife is not his wife but a common-law partner."

"That we've suspected. Listen, if this is the man, then you need to be very careful. He has eyes and ears all over town."

"I am aware of that, Jake. Find him. Find out if he's the one. Kitlin can't take much more of this. And neither can I." Avery watched as Jake nodded before they both walked back to the front door. "I'll be in touch."

Avery closed and locked the front door, hearing faint conversation on the other side of it before the vehicles drove away. This had not been what he needed. He yawned as he headed back for his office, turning off lights on the way there. He would sleep in his office tonight. He just couldn't get undressed and sleep in his own bed. His thoughts were that troubled.

Chapter 32

Avery rose and stretched the next day, his shift finished. He headed for the office, intent on planning his next day's list of songs and having it ready to go before he left. He had been working on it over the day, as he usually did.

Pausing at the doorway to the reception area, he looked around. He missed Kitlin there. He hadn't had a chance to speak with her, not that day, but she had sent him a text. She had missed him last night and that worried her. Was he okay? He had smiled and returned her text, adding a couple of hearts as he did so.

Kitlin laid her phone aside, snuggling down as best she could under the covers. She was falling in love, she knew, but she worried about Avery, about his safety. She didn't know why it was happening but it was. Would she have met him otherwise? She would like to think that she had, but she won't even sure about that.

Kieren approached his sister the next morning, knowing that she was feeling bored but also not well enough to do much. He set a pad of paper and pen beside her.

"Kieren? What's this for?"

"Write down what you are thinking. What you know. What you think. What you want to happen. You know that's what Dad always tells us to do."

"I know. I'm afraid of that, though, Kieren. I just don't understand why." Kitlin leaned back against her couch back.

"We know that you are. Listen, Avery is at work. He'll be here after work and I know that his parents will be here too. Dad and Mom asked them. They want to start working on this. Dad wants this over for you. So do Michael and Meg."

"I'm not up to that many people here. At least, I don't think I am." Kitlin looked down at the paper, her pen drawing doodles on it. "Kieren, where would you start?"

"Where would I start?" He rose, heading for his laptop, returning to sit beside her. "With a map. Do you know where you were kept captive?"

Kitlin nodded.

"I do. There's a folder on my desk. It has some information in it, as well as the house where we were." Kitlin watched as Kieren retrieved it. "Now, we know that it was on the outskirts of town, just enough into the country to be isolated. Kieren, that friend of yours? The one who does title searches?"

"Samuel? Sure. I can ask him to look into this. He'll do that. His father as well can look into the financials once he has a name." Kieren sent off a quick text message, finding Samuel returning it rapidly. "He'll look into it. He had already had that thought but didn't have the address."

"Now what?" Kitlin was writing rapidly, trying to get her thoughts down. "We think it's someone high in town."

"That would make sense. He would be able to hide in plain sight, as they say." Kieren was on his feet, his eyes on the clock, returning with sandwiches and juice for them both, Kitlin's medications on the tray.

"I don't want the heavy stuff, Kieren. Just something over the counter."

"That's what there. You need to take it." Kieren bit into his sandwich, chewed and swallowed his food. "Avery said that he had a parcel left at his home last night. Just a note and a stuffed toy of some kind. Jake came out to get it. It has them puzzled. Jake didn't say what the note said."

"He should. It involves both of us."

"I'm sure that he will with time. He wants to meet with us all tonight, if he can make it."

"I'm tired of meeting with him. Of just talking. We need to end this and now."

"And we will. Now, your bodyguards are around, are they not?"

Kitlin shook her head.

"I refused. I told them to go home. That having them around made me feel as if I was a captive again."

Kieren looked shocked at that and then nodded. That's exactly how she would feel. He could understand her thinking. Only how did they keep her safe?

Chapter 33

Avery watched Streeter closely that afternoon. He had finished his time on the radio, set what he needed for the next day, and then headed to find his boss. He just wanted to touch base with him, to ensure that all was well.

Streeter looked up as he heard Avery's footsteps and waved him into the office, pointing to a chair. Avery sat, his head dropping and his eyes closing. He had not slept well that night, Jake contacting him about an hour after he had left. He dozed off briefly, his head jerking up as he felt a hand on his shoulder and heard a mug set on the desk in front of him.

Streeter chose to sit in a chair beside Avery, his own mug of coffee in his hand. He watched his young friend closely, knowing how fatigued that Avery was.

"Avery? What can you tell me?"

Avery rubbed at his eyes and then scrubbed his hands down his face. He heard the sounds of music wafting through the building, his thoughts distracted by the tune for a moment. He then studied Streeter's desk, seeing the neat piles of paper and unopened envelopes on it.

"I don't know, Streeter. I told you about the package from last night. Jake said the note simply said that they would be in touch. What we don't understand is the stuffed toy."

———

"Stuffed toy? That makes me think that this goes back to when you were young, a baby or toddler. Would that be your thinking?"

Avery nodded, having come to that conclusion himself.

"I talked to Dad on my break. He gave me a name but I'm not sure about it. He's really up in the town businesses." Avery took a sideways look at Streeter.

Streeter nodded, having come to that conclusion. He simply said a name, seeing Avery's eyes closed.

"That's who Dad said. How do we prove it?" Avery was desperate to have this over. He wanted to spend Christmas with his lady if she would let him without this hanging over them.

"We do our footwork. Jake has to prove it as does Frankie. We can work away on it, just as your friends all have. Abe has mentioned that Emma had a name that she was searching and that his men were working on this. Kieren has reached out to a friend of his who does title searches and has given him the address where you were held. That's making it work. Now, what do we do with you? You need to sleep and you're not."

"No, I'm not. And I won't take anything for it. I just need to make sure that Kitlin is safe."

"And you can't do that when you're not together." Streeter watched with compassion as Avery nodded, wiping at the tears on his cheeks. "You can't be together, not as you would like. Greg has approached me, you know. He has suggested that you two marry, but you're not ready to take that step. Neither one of you are. We'll figure it out. You can spend the late afternoons and evenings together. Kitlin is adamant that she is coming back to work next week. I'll allow it. It's not a difficult position and she should be okay."

"I know. She told Richard that she didn't want any bodyguards at this point. I can't say as I blame her."

"I would have done the same thing." Streeter paused, not sure how to continue. "Avery, you are one of the best hosts that we have. What are your thoughts about your future?"

"My future? I figured on staying here for as long as I can. Why would you ask that?" Avery was puzzled, not sure where Streeter was heading with his question.

"I want to run something by you. Pray about it. Becky and I are looking to retire at some point. We would like to offer you the radio station, for you to come in a partner for now. I don't want an answer today. There is no timeline in fact for you to answer."

Avery was floored, not having expected this at all. He nodded before he rose. He had a lot to think about and pray about. He gathered his coat and travel mug and headed outside, looking around for his escort. He didn't see them and turned back to the building. Avery froze in place, his mug dropping to the pavement. His hands rose in the air. Avery stood for a moment, watching the gun held on him before he turned and walked away from the building, heading for a vehicle parked near the entrance of the parking lot. He prayed that his abduction would be caught on the security stream.

Shoved into the truck, his hands were bound and then a blindfold was tied tightly over his eyes. He grew afraid before he began to pray. He had no idea who the men were or where he was heading.

Kitlin paced her apartment an hour later. Avery had promised to be there thirty minutes ago and he hadn't appeared. Michael approached, a frown on his face.

"Kitlin? Avery said he would be here?" His arm rested around her shoulders to keep her still.

"He did. And he's not. Where is he?" Kitlin sent another text off to Avery, waiting for a response and not getting one. "Michael? What happened?"

"I don't know." Michael walked away, his phone out, shaking his head at Paul and Kieren. "Frankie? Avery was to be at Kitlin's thirty minutes ago. He hasn't shown up. I just found out when he was to be here."

Frankie's hand froze as he held his pen before he threw it down, his jacket in his hand as he ran for his vehicle. He had a bad feeling about this. Turning into the parking lot, his lights still flashing but the siren stopped, he flung open his door and ran for the building. Sliding to a halt, he stared down at the coffee mug on the ground. It was Avery's, he knew, and that meant that Avery had more than likely disappeared again. This was not to have happened. Lord, protect this friend. Bring him back safely.

Chapter 34

Frankie searched the parking lot, having called in patrol officers to help. He stared at the camera over the back door, a hand reaching up for a moment. He sighed. It had been blacked out. Micah stood near him, having come in at Frankie's call.

"They blacked it out?" Micah shook his head. "I didn't know that. I'm sorry, Frankie. We were just finishing up with the training for today. I haven't had a chance to check the feed since noon."

"Not your fault, Micah. This is a sophisticated group, one who seems to be one step ahead of us at all times." Frankie stopped speaking, a thought coming to him. Lord, not that again. Not another officer on the take.

"You suspect someone on the force. I would find it strange if there wasn't. Emma's finding information on this man that gives her concern."

"I know. I spoke with her about an hour ago." Frankie pulled the door open and headed for Streeter, who stood watching them. "Streeter, what time did Avery leave?"

"About an hour ago. He was late getting away. He spent some time talking business with me. No sign of him?"

"Other than his coffee mug, no." Frankie turned in a circle, knowing that they would need to search the building as well. "We'll need to search in here, Streeter. They blacked out the camera at the door."

"I see. That doesn't surprise me, knowing who is likely involved. When you're done, come and find me. We need to talk." Streeter walked away, his shoulders hunched slightly from the weight of what he knew.

"He's hurting, Frankie." Micah walked away, his phone out to call Abe. He turned back. "Avery's guards? Where are they?"

Frankie nodded. He had had the same thought.

"We'll look for them. I don't know where they are. They should be here." Frankie turned as he heard his name called and walked that way to where Jake stood waiting for him.

Kieren stepped back from the doorway, his eyes on Frankie and Jake as they walked down the hallway towards him. He sighed. Avery had disappeared. This is going to hurt Kitlin really bad.

"Guys?" He pointed into the apartment. "Kitlin is pacing. She is sure something has happened to Avery."

Frankie nodded, his jacket flung on a chair before he turned to face the two sets of parents and the siblings who waited for him. Aubrey and Aveleen and their spouses had arrived as well. He felt the apartment was getting small. He had spoken with Abe, who had suggested that they move Kitlin and Kieren to a cabin at his compound. That way, they could provide better security for her. Both men were afraid that the abductors would appear and hurt someone else in the building.

"I'm sorry, Michael, Meg, Kitlin. Everyone. Avery has disappeared. He disappeared after he left work. In fact, his guards have disappeared as well. We don't know at this point who has him or where he actually is." He paused, hearing the strangled sob from Kitlin and the crumpling on the faces of the other ladies.

Michael wrapped an arm around his wife, his own face growing stern.

"What can we do to help find him? We're not sitting still this time, Frankie."

"No, we didn't think that you would. I need to go back to the office, but we would like to make some changes. Abe has suggested that we move you all out to his compound. Or at least move Kitlin and Kieren. They will go after her to get Avery to cooperate with them. After all, they are a couple, aren't they?" His grin briefly crossed his face as the others gave soft laughs.

Kitlin frowned at him. They weren't a couple, she thought. And would never be.

"I see, Frankie. Do we have any choice in that?"

"You do. Think about. If it comes to it, Caleb will move you to somewhere more secure. That's a given. You won't have a choice at that time." Frankie stayed for a few more moments before he walked away, nodding at Jake as he did so.

———

Jake turned back to the group. He was with them for now, Caleb sending him that way. He wanted a police officer with them and felt a detective was the best. That way, Jake could work with them.

"Jake, where do we go from here?" Aubrey, Logan, and Kieren had approached, Paul and Michael behind them.

"For now, prayer. Then, we'll talk. I want all of you to write down any impressions, thoughts, ideas, whatever. Then, we'll combine them. Micah is on his way back here with Kat. She has information that she needs to verify. Doug's team is around outside for tonight. Kitlin, I'm sorry. I'm sorry that we couldn't keep Avery safe for you. But as of now, you are in police protective custody. That means we will move you, just as Frankie has said."

Kitlin nodded, moving through the crowd, heading for the front window. She stood, the drapes cracked open slightly, stifling back sobs. She felt an arm around her and then another. Aveleen and Finlee had found her and shared the watch with her. For on watch for Avery was exactly what she was doing.

"Ladies, what can we do? We can't just sit here. I know that we can pray, but there has to be something more that we are capable of doing."

"There is." Kataleen had arrived, sheafs of papers in her hands. "We'll pray and then we'll work through this. Your mom is putting on pots of coffee and tea, Kitlin. Meg is preparing sandwiches. Rylee sent in treats for us. So we'll have nourishment to keep going."

———

"I like how you think. Okay, so let's get started."
Kitlin sat, her arm and shoulder being to ache. Kieren
simply handed her an ice pack and pain medications.
She nodded, her eyes on Michael.   He's up to
something, she thought.

Chapter 35

A day later, Caleb turned from his computer. He was disturbed, to say the least. A friend from another force had reached out to him. Andrew McBeth, Greenton police chief, had called, for one thing just to catch up, but he had information from an informant in his town. He was heading Riverville way and asked that he could meet with Caleb and whichever detective was working the case of Avery and Kitlin. He refused to say why, simply that it was better that they talk in person.

"Frankie? Andrew McBeth will be here in about an hour. He's on the road heading this way. He wants to meet with us about Avery and Kitlin." Caleb stood in Frankie's office doorway, his eyes taking in the stress on his friend's face.

"Andrew? That's odd. Did he say why?" Frankie looked up at that.

"No, just that it was better to meet in person. I'll make sure the small boardroom is free and clear." A grim look was on Caleb's face. They had begun daily sweeping of the offices, which had paid off. They had found listening devices in the hallway, but not the offices. Jake and another trusted officer were going back over the tapes from there to determine just who had placed them.

"Okay. Let me know when he arrives. I have some calls to make to follow up on that murder."

Frankie sat back and then beckoned Caleb into the office.

Caleb entered, closing the door and then standing against it. He knew Frankie well enough know that he had an idea and needed to gather his thoughts first before he spoke.

"We know that we have a mole here in the detachment. And there are likely moles in other government offices. It would not make sense if there weren't. We have enough that we can start making arrests. But those we arrest will not turn on those above them."

"Not likely. They usually don't." Caleb waited patiently, his own thoughts troubled.

"So, how do we flush them out without giving away our hand? There has to be a way." Frankie looked down at his phone and read the text message. "Micah has found out who sprayed the security camera. It was George Tait."

"George?" Caleb mulled the name. "Of course, he's related to her. A nephew if I remember correctly."

"And he is likely one of our leaks. We can arrest for tampering with the camera. I would be glad to do that."

"No, I need you here. Jake is with our group. Pull in Amy. She can do that. And keep it quiet. He's not working today, so we may need to search for him. Have her pull the search warrants as well."

———

Frankie nodded as he rose to find Amy, sending her on her way. Her shocked look turned to one of determination.

Andrew dropped his briefcase on the table in the boardroom before he turned, his jacket off and on the back of a chair. This would not be easy, he knew. It never was when fellow officers were involved.

"Andrew? It's good to see you again." Frankie handed him a mug of coffee. "I know. It seems that all we do is drink coffee."

"That it does. Other than Caleb here who prefers tea." Andrew sat, a prayer rising within him. "Can we pray first, fellows? This is going to be difficult enough."

Caleb reached for the paperwork that Andrew was handing him, their time of prayer finished.

"What have you found, Andrew?"

"Bill Buckley was working on a case and came across that information. He knew it didn't belong with the man who he arrested for murder. But it does involve your town. And Avery and Kitlin. I know Avery through Aubrey. This material? It involves someone in your town."

"We're getting that sense. Only we don't have the proof that we need to arrest him." Frankie was frustrated. He had spent time with Kitlin that day and hadn't been able to ease her fears or doubts.

"We understand. This should help somewhat in that way. And I understand Emma is hard at work as are her employees. "

———

"She is." Caleb read through the material. "This is a lot of new material, I suspect. Frankie, Jake is with Kitlin for now. Pull Amy in on this. She'll be good. She thinks outside of the box, more so than you do."

"That she does." Frankie looked around, trying to make sense of it all.

"I won't stay much longer, fellows. I wanted to bring you this myself. Bill would have but he's in court today." Andrew was away at that.

Caleb looked back through the material, picking it apart as he knew Frankie was doing.

"I'll need to speak with Michael and Meg about this. They may have more information."

"And talk to Ben and Eddie. They have both offered to help. Ben likely can given us more information that what we can use."

"They were next. Where do you think Avery is?" Frankie looked up as Caleb remained silent.

"I wish I knew. Hannah is hurting, having another cousin disappear. And she hasn't had a name or reason yet. This is one time that I would welcome God using her this way." Caleb was on his feet, heading for his office. He had paperwork waiting for him that wouldn't get itself done.

Frankie looked around as Amy appeared beside him, reaching to sit. He didn't like the look on her face.

"Amy?"

"We were too late, Frankie. George is dead. And it wasn't at his own hand."

"Murdered, to keep him quiet. The team's working through it?"

"They are. I'm heading back there. I just wanted to update you in person."

Chapter 36

Kitlin turned as she heard the apartment door open and close. She knew that the person who she most wished to walk in would not be the one who had just entered. Frankie's voice came to her as he spoke to Kieren and then her father.

"Kitlin?" She turned as Frankie came up behind her.

"Frankie? Any word?" Her heart fell as he shook his head.

"Not yet. We're working on it. I just wanted to update you on what we have discovered today. The man who sprayed the security camera was identified as a police officer. Unfortunately, we can't question him. One of our detectives was sent to bring him in and found him dead."

"Murdered? They're taking out their own people? What does that mean for Avery?" Kitlin's hand covered her eyes. "What else?"

"Friends from a police force in another town have had word about you two. The police chief made a trip today to bring us that information. We're working on verifying it, but I can tell you that it confirms some of our suspicions."

"It does? And how does that help solve this and bring Avery home?" Kitlin grew hopeful at that.

"It does help. It moves the investigation along. We're looking into who their employees are and who their contacts are. I know that it feels like a slow process but we'll get there." Frankie looked around as he heard a phone chiming, knowing that it wasn't his.

Kitlin reached for her phone that Kieren was handing her. She frowned at the notification of a message from a number that she didn't recognize. She brought up the message, a hand across her mouth as sobs began. Her hand was shaking as she thrust her phone at Frankie. Crumpling to the floor, Kitlin buried her head in her arms, sobs wracking her body.

Frankie stared at her and then at her phone. This is not good, was his thought, before he forwarded the message to himself and then to a trusted crime scene tech who was working that night.

Kieren approached, his hand on Kitlin's phone. He stared at the photo. It was Avery, but it wasn't just a picture of Avery. He had been beaten, that much was obvious. But it was the surroundings that drew their attention. Rock walls and rough flooring, rock, Kieren thought. Where is he? Another underground cell?

"Do you recognize this place, Frankie?" Kieren's voice was hushed, not sure if he should even ask.

"Not offhand, but it's in the area, I'm sure. They'll want to stay close, to keep an eye on Kitlin. We're going to have to move you two. I would take her phone, but I won't. That's how they'll keep in contact with her. Only, I don't know how many of these pictures she can handle seeing."

"She's stronger than you think, Frankie. She'll cope with whatever is sent her way. I know that her faith has been wavering but it's coming back stronger. She told me that she felt like a pauper who suddenly had a wealth of whatever she needed set in front of her. That God had promised that she and Avery would get through this. That He had promised never to leave her or forsake her. She is clinging to that."

Kitlin was on her feet, Kieren reaching to wrap an arm around his sister.

"Frankie? How do we respond? They just sent that picture but no message. Isn't that odd?"

"Not really. They're trying to play mind games with you. And this is part of how they do that. Pictures with no messages. I would suspect that you'll get a message next. We'll need to move you somewhere, Kitlin." He stood, shock on his face, as she walked away. "Did she just do that?"

"She did, Frankie. She's not leaving. Not now. She'll want to be where Avery can find her. That would be here." Kieren knew that his sister had not walked that far away. He stared at the kitchen window, seeing the grey skies overhead.

"She needs to stay safe. How can that happen if she walks away from us?" Frustrated, Frankie left as well, heading for the office and hopefully some news that would move the investigation along.

Kitlin appeared in front of Kieren, her arms wrapped around herself. Her shoulder was aching, but she did not want to take anything for it. She needed her wits about her, she decided. Today was the day, the day that she went through everything that she had and solved this.

Kieren watched his sister over the day, providing meals and coffee for her. He finally reached to take the paperwork from her, despite her protest.

"You need to rest, sis. Avery would want you to do that."

Kitlin sighed and agreed.

"He would. I just wish I knew where he was. He's hurt and needs care." Kitlin took with a quiet word of thanks the mug of hot chocolate that he handed her.

"I understand that, Kitlin. But he would want you to take care of yourself." Kieren moved aside piles of paper to sit beside her. His hand reached for hers as he bent to pray for the couple. "Now, let's set this aside for tonight. You'll think better after a break."

"I guess. I just need to solve this."

"And we will." Kieren stared around the living room, seeing the small touches that his sister had used to try and make it home. "You're not happy here, are you?"

"Here? As in the apartment?" Kitlin shook her head. "No, it's not home. I tried to make it that, but it just isn't. I don't know where that is any more."

Kieren turned his head, his eyes thoughtful.

"Your home is where Avery is. We can all see that. We'll find him, Kitlin, and bring him back to

———

you." Kieren rose at last and headed for bed, admonishing his sister to do the same.

Kitlin watched him head for bed before she was on her feet, cleaning the kitchen, setting another pot of coffee, and then heading for a shower. Dressed in her comfy clothes as she called them, she poured a cup of coffee and headed back for her office, turning to stare at the piles of paper in the living room. Sudden determination filled her as she reached for all the papers and set them on the kitchen table. She would work until she solved this, and solve this she would.

Chapter 37

Paper littered almost every surface in the apartment by the next morning. Kitlin rubbed at her tired, red eyes. She had worked overnight, sorting through what they had found themselves, what Emma had provided. Samuel had been in touch, sending even more paperwork as had his father. Abe's men had been in touch as well, sending what they had. Kat had provided a family tree, such as she was able to release to her.

Kieren stood in the kitchen, studying that table before he stepped back to the living room, studying the piles of paperwork covering the surfaces there. He reached for a piece of paper on top of one pile, nodding at the neat notes that Kitlin had placed there.

Kitlin stood behind her brother, her eyes on him before she reached to take the paper from him, replacing it. She stood for a moment, lost in thought. She didn't see her brother studying her and then nodding.

Seeing the determination in his sister, Kieren simply reached to hug her. There was a lightness in her spirit that he had not seen for months, since before she moved. Kitlin was back and ready to fight.

"What happened, Kitlin?"

"What happened? This? I just started putting it all together. I hadn't planned on staying up all night. It's making sense, Kieren. Finally, it's making sense.

———

I'll go over it with you. That is, if you're up to it." She sent him a smirk, bringing a grin to his face. "And yes, my shoulder is sore, but not as sore as it was."

"Okay. We eat. Then, we'll go through this. Do you want to bring anyone else in?" Kieren reached for bread to make them toast.

"Not for now. Frankie sent a text message this morning, just warning me to be careful." Kitlin turned from the stove, setting the bacon and eggs on their plates and then reaching for the orange juice.

Their meal finished and the remnants cleared away, Kieren walked through the house, stopping to read the notes on each pile of paper. She's good, he thought. Logical, concise, getting right to the heart of it all.

Kitlin moved through the house, her thoughts troubled. She prayed for her friend, Avery, and that he would be home soon. Only she didn't think that he would be. Her greatest fear that he would be returned only for them to have a funeral for him. She had had to pray that through over the night hours and release him.

Kieren reached for another piece of paper, his hand freezing as he read it. He pulled Kitlin back towards him, his mouth opening and closing without any words coming from it.

"Kieren? What is it?" She tilted his hand to read the paper. "Her? Yes, she's from our town but moved here years ago. She's related to the one in charge. A sister, I think Kataleen has determined."

"So, our town is involved in this?" Kieren was shocked for moment.

"It would appear so. Now, what do we do with all this?" Kitlin turned to head for the door, opening it to find Michael and Meg and her own parents standing there. "You're all here? Do you have news?"

"No, we don't." Michael spoke for the group before they all reached to hug her, moving past to comment on the piles of paper. "What have you done, you two?"

"It's not me. It's Kitlin's fault." Kieren grinned as his sister made a face at him. "She's been working overnight. I walked out to all these piles of paper."

"You did, did you, son?" Paul walked through the apartment, reading the notes. "You've numbered each pile, Kitlin. Any reason why?"

"There is. I numbered and numbered them over and over. They are in logical order, by date and then by location and event. I didn't realize I had so much information." Kitlin stood, her hands on her face, as she stared at them.

"Have you draw any conclusions?" Esther wrapped an arm around her daughter.

"I have. I don't like it." Distress coloured her face.

"She's tracked a relative of the top guy back to our town, Dad. A sister, I think she said."

"He's from our town?" Paul was shocked, turning as he heard the door opening again and the two younger couples walked in, heading for the kitchen with their bag before their coats were off and they stood with them.

"No, he's not. She lived there when she was in her early twenties but moved back here. They are from this town. I couldn't trace them back to the early days of founding the town, just to their parents. Kat has done a lot of work on that as well." Kitlin turned to Aubrey and Logan. "You're all here. Now, we need to put this all together and make sense of it."

"Okay, Kitlin. We'll start with putting it onto a program on the computer and then set up a database. Does that work?" Aubrey grinned at her nod. "Lead me to your computer."

"Laptop. I've started a list. You can work on that. What we need is for this to be divided up and have some of you read back through each pile. Make your own notes. Emma said that she would have more for us today. Only, she wasn't sure just when. Micah and Kat will be around later today. And Darcy is moving in on us after lunch, she said."

"Lots of help, love." Paul reached to hug his daughter, before he stood hands on her shoulders. "You need to rest, Kitlin."

"I will, Dad. I just need to solve this. And Frankie will not be happy with me. I know that."

"And why would that be?" Logan watched her closely, seeing the fear that she was trying too hard to hide.

"Because I'm doing his work."

———

"Not really. You're researching on your own adventure. They can't stop you from doing that. We'll give him what we have when we're done and they will then confirm it all." Logan walked away, heading for the office, hearing Michael and Kieren talking.

"He's right." Aveleen reached to wrap an arm around Kitlin. "You're family now, Kitlin. We help our family. Friends do the same. Hannah has asked if she can be involved as well. She suspected that you were up to something."

"She did? That's right. You're cousins." Kitlin looked around. "I don't have enough room here to host everyone."

"No, you don't. But we'll manage. At some point, we'll move you from here." Michael had appeared once more. "The plan is to move you to somewhere safe, clear out your apartment, and make it look as if you have disappeared. That may cause problems for my son, but it will keep you safe."

Kitlin looked at him, horrified for a moment, but then nodding. That made sense, she decided. Only, she wasn't sure that she was ready for that. Hearing a slight noise, she turned, sensing a new person in the room but seeing no one. *Who was here? Lord, is that our angel once more? Come to protect me? Come to help us solve this?*

Chapter 38

By afternoon, there had been a consensus reached. Kitlin moved around her apartment, her eyes on the group gathered there. It had grown over the day, with Frankie and Jake dropping in for a while. Micah had shown up as had Joseph and Luke from his team. Greg and Mary, their pastor and his wife, were there as well. To say that she felt overwhelmed would have been an understatement. Emma had watched her and then just moved her to the bedroom, shutting the door and sitting beside her. Kitlin could hear the prayer raised for her and felt relief. She was not on her own, living through this. She had family and friends.

"Emma, where do we go from here?"

"We give Frankie and Jake a copy of what you have discovered. Don't worry. We'll give him copies of it all. Luke and Joseph are working on that, scanning everything and then downloading it onto a thumb drive. Then, we spend the next hours in prayer." Emma bit at her lip, uncertainty n her face for a moment. "Did your dad talk to you about moving?"

"He did. I can see why, but I'm afraid that Avery won't be able to find me."

"He will. We'll make sure of that. He would want you safe above anything else. Have you received any more messages?" Emma had seen the original message. It distressed her but she had totally expected that.

"No, I haven't. Just that one." Kitlin blinked. "Did you see it?"

"I did. And I have seen much more brutal photos."

"Did you recognize anything about where he is?"

Emma shook her head, knowing what Kitlin had been asking.

"No, I didn't. We can look into it, but I don't think that we have enough information to determine where he is being kept. Frankie will be tracing back to what phone was used."

"If he can. Don't they usually use pay-as-you-go phones for this?"

Emma laughed at the plaintive tone in Kitlin's voice.

"They should do. But sometimes they don't do that. And that is what our prayer is. That they have used a phone that we can trace. And Frankie will not tell you if that's the case."

"About what I figured. He can't." Kitlin looked around. "When do I have to move?"

"Not tonight. Tonight? You sleep. You need to. You were up all last night." Emma rose, her hand on Kitlin's shoulder. "Go to sleep, Kitlin. We'll be here when you awaken. We're not walking away from you. We don't do that to our friends."

Kitlin yawned, her eyes watering as she did so.

"Has Richard forgiven me for sending him away?"

Emma began to laugh, bringing Kitlin's eyes to her.

"He has. And he has never left. His team has been here all along. He's friends with the couple across the hall. They've been there all along."

"They have been? I will owe so many people so much." Kitlin's head found her pillow as she drifted off.

Emma pulled a blanket over her new friend, prayers raising for her.

"Not a penny, my friend. You will owe no one anything. That's a guarantee and a promise."

Emma walked towards Abe, into his hug, before she turned to watch the activity. The piles of papers had been stacked neatly into labelled file folders and set on a table in the office. She could hear the conversation and laughter coming from the kitchen as a meal was prepared.

"She's asleep, Abe." Emma leaned back against Abe, reliving the adventures of their friends and themselves.

"She needs that. Kieren said that she hasn't been sleeping."

"No, she won't. We know what that was like. She asked when she had to move?"

"Soon. Right now, we think that she's okay. Any more messages?"

———

"Not that she has said. She said the one yesterday has been the only one. Kitlin did ask if I recognized where he was being held."

"We can't. There is not enough information to do that. Micah is working on trying to trace back to the number, but he says it looks as if it was a spoofed number."

"That figures. What else can we do for them?" Emma was thinking through scenarios and ways to help.

"Right at the moment? Not a lot. Frankie said they're at a standstill but thanked us for what we have been able to forward." Abe looked around. "We need to leave, Emma. Isaac has that party tonight that we're to be at and it's cutting it close."

"That it is." Emma and Abe walked away, feeling as if they were abandoning Kitlin.

Kitlin rose late that night, finding her parents and Avery's parents still there, working through what they had discovered. She accepted their hugs and then grabbed her jacket and walked outside. She heard footsteps beside her, thinking that it was Kieren.

"How are you, Kitlin?" Richard's voice startled her for a moment.

"I'm not sure how to feel. Is that honest enough for you?"

Richard grinned, knowing that Kitlin was baiting him.

"It is, Kitlin. And about how we would expect you to feel. Did you accomplish anything overnight?"

———

Kitlin shrugged, not quite sure how he knew that she had been up all night.

"Before you ask, we do rounds outside every little while. We saw your light on all night. We thought that you would be working through this."

"Richard, what are your thoughts? You know Avery. You know this town. What is the motive here?"

Richard nodded. Kitlin had gone to the centre of the very mystery.

"That is a good question. I would think that it goes back to when Avery was young. You've become involved just because you were there. We haven't seen any evidence that your families knew one another before all this. Now, your father? It could involve him because of his work, but we doubt that. That's the word we're getting from the streets. That you were taken just because you were there. They couldn't let you stay, not to give a statement and perhaps identify them. When you two walked away, you threw them off their game. They're playing catch up. Only you two aren't cooperating by being out by yourself." Richard paused to gather his thoughts. "When you were taken on Saturday? That was an attempt to get to Avery, to make him play their games. Only you messed that up."

"I really did, didn't I?" Kitlin grinned up at Richard. "Now, how do we plan to catch these people?"

———

Chapter 39

Frankie turned as he heard his name called, his steps slowing as Aubrey ran to catch up with him. He had no news for his friend, and that disturbed him.

"Frankie? Heading to Mac's?"

Frankie grinned back at Aubrey.

"I am. And so are you. But you have something for me." Frankie took the thumb drive offered to him, tucking it into a pocket.

"That is the summary of what we have found. We finished up last night and then loaded it up for you." Aubrey nodded at Mac as they walked towards a booth at the back of the cafe. "We pray that it helps. There has been no word?"

"None. We suspect that Avery is held here somewhere in town or close to it. There just hasn't been anyone who has seen him. And that is very unusual."

"It is. Your sources usually are on this, aren't they?"

"They are. And I wish that they would come forward. Every day that Avery is missing is a day that he is in more danger."

"I don't think so, Frankie. They won't do anything. Not yet. They're building up to something and that leads up to Christmas. What big events are coming up?"

Frankie shook his head. Aubrey had just asked a question that they had all been struggling with.

"We looked at that, Aubrey. I can't go into details on that, as you know." He looked up as Mac appeared beside them, sliding over to let him sit. "Mac?"

"You're looking for him. I know that, Frankie. Here. This was left for you today." Mac handed over a dirt-smudged envelope. He would never say who left it there, even though he knew that it was an undercover officer who had handed it to him. No one could explain how Mac knew these officers.

Frankie looked at the envelope before he tucked it away.

"What are you hearing, Mac?"

"Not a lot. Like you, I'm not being talked to. That tells me that either they have been threatened or else they don't know anything."

"I suspect that they have been threatened. They've kept quiet before, just to protect us. I wish that they would speak."

Aubrey nodded, knowing that Frankie was right. They needed someone to come forward. Only it didn't appear that they would.

"Kieren has some information that he is confirming with a friend. He has tracked through the house and the companies involved in it through a friend. This friend's father has done a forensics search as has Gideon. They are putting together the final pieces and said they would have those today."

"Okay. Tell him to come and find me when he has it all." Frankie sighed as his phone rang, watching Mac moving around among the diners. He read his text and then stuffed the phone away again. This call wasn't urgent. Just a request from a friend to meet him.

"What has Ben had to say?" Aubrey sipped at his coffee, his eyes trained outside the window.

"Not a lot. He and Marg are heading out of town for a week or so, to a conference. He has left some names for me to follow up on. Eddie has been away as well, just back tomorrow. I'll talk to him, but they're not on the force any more. This is when I wish that they were."

"I would think so. But they were ready to retire. They needed that." Aubrey sighed. "I just wish I knew where he was. I'd go in and find him and bring him home."

"We all would." Frankie stood at last and walked away, leaving Aubrey to sit and contemplate life.

Aubrey looked up as he sensed someone sliding into the booth across from him. He didn't know the couple but they seemed to know him.

"Do I know you?" His words held an unspoken question.

"No, you don't. Not yet. But Kieren said I'd find you here when I spoke to him early. I'm Samuel and this is my wife, Aideen. We're the friends who do the title searching."

—————

"Of course." Aubrey looked up for Mac, finding him already heading his way. "Let's eat, it's that close to lunch. Then, I'll take you to find Kieren and Kitlin."

Tapping at Kitlin's door a while later, Aubrey shook his head as Samuel grinned at him. Samuel had simply commented that they had found plenty of information that he had had a friend on the police in his town confirm.

Kieren opened the door, surprised to see the trio.

"Come on in. Kitlin's not here right now. She's away with Dad and Mom."

"That's okay. Samuel here said that they had information for you." Aubrey shrugged out of his coat. "Now, what do we have?"

Samuel simply shook his head.

"He's impatient, Kieren. You didn't tell us that."

Kieren laughed.

"He is. He's had an adventure, just like you two. And I have told him about it. Now, what do you have?"

"About what you asked me to find." Samuel handed over a folder. "Here are the copies of what we found. You are our client, not the police. It is up to you what you share with them. I will say that Bill Buckley has confirmed everything for us. If you want him to reach out to the force here, he can do that. I took that step, knowing what we were facing."

"Thank you, Samuel. Let's go through this and see what we have." Kieren started reading, handing over a copy to Aubrey. "This is bad, you know. He really does control things in some ways here in town."

"He does. And that is concerning. That is why I went to Bill and asked for that." Samuel shared a look with Aideen.

"I see. Okay. We'll need to speak with Kitlin first before we do anything. And she's not due back for a while. How long can you two stay for?"

"Not too much longer. We have a commitment this evening that we need to be at."

Kieren shut the door behind his friends, his thoughts troubled. Aubrey had had to leave some time earlier, leaving Kieren on his own. He turned as he heard a sound at the door, thinking that it was Kitlin. Only it wasn't. When the door closed again, Kieren lay in a bloody, crumpled heap on the hall floor.

———

Chapter 40

Tapping at Kitlin's door, Stephen frowned. He had been told that she was home, only there was no answer. A sudden thought had him trying the door handle, shocked to find it twisting under his hand and the door opening.

"Kitlin? Kieren? Are you here? Hey, are either one of you here?" Stephen reached for the light switch, dusk having fallen. His eyes dropped to Kieren before he was on his knees, a hand reaching to assess him.

On his feet, he was across the hall, the door open to call for Richard and Silver who were on duty inside. Timothy and Naomi were due back in a couple of hours.

"Richard? Kieren's down. We need emergency services." He was gone almost before he finished his words, his hands back to assess how badly hurt Kieren was. Blood covered his hand as he reached to touch Kieren's head and face.

Standing back against the hallway wall, Stephen rubbed at his hands, trying to remove the blood. Richard stood beside him, grim looks on both the faces. Silver had headed for the parking lot, knowing that Kitlin was due back about that time.

"How bad is he?" Richard's quiet question cut through the strained silence, the quiet words of the paramedics not reaching to them. He looked around at the activity surrounding them.

"I don't know. He's not conscious. How did this happen, Richard? We're right across the hall."

"But we're not watching the door constantly. That's what happened. And we need to change that. We're needing to be away next week. Don's moving in to cover for us. Kitlin won't have a choice now about moving to someone more secure. This has been brought to her home."

"I know." Stephen looked around as a patrol officer approached them. "I have given my statement, officer. Do you need something more?"

The officer nodded.

"I understand that one of you will be riding with Kieren?" At Richard's nod, he pointed to the door. "They're about ready to go. Just follow them. It's been cleared for you to ride with them." He watched as Stephen walked away. "Richard? You're staying here?"

"I am. I have someone with Kitlin at the moment. My other two team members are on their way in. I gather that she's not going to be able to access her apartment for a while."

The officer shook his head, even as he turned to stare back in the door.

"Not for a while. Not before tomorrow. We have to go through the whole place. Frankie and Jake are on their way."

"Figured that they would be. Have Frankie call me when he gets here. I'm moving Kitlin to the hospital for now. Her parents are here too."

———

"Will do." The officer watched Richard walk away. Richard was well known in the law enforcement community. He didn't think that he had even seen the slump to Richard's shoulders that showed for just a few moments.

Frankie tracked Stephen down late that night. Stephen had stationed himself outside Kieren's door and refused to move. He nodded at Frankie before Timothy moved in to take over his spot.

"Stephen. Come with me. You need to eat. And I know I could use something." Frankie waited until they had finished their sandwiches before he spoke again. "How are you?"

"Frustrated. Hurting for Kitlin and her parents. I have spoken with Kieren. He doesn't know who did it. He really doesn't remember a lot."

"No, he won't. I am just thankful that he wasn't killed." Frankie sipped at his coffee. "What can you tell me?"

"Not a lot more than what I said in my statement. I had gone over to check on them, just like we have been. I had a feeling something had happened. You know those feelings. When the door knob turned under my hand, I knew something was wrong." Stephen stopped speaking, his mind going back to that moment, his eyes searching through the cafe, not seeing many people there. "I have no idea who it was."

"We get that. I just needed to speak with you to see what else you had remembered." Frankie rose, heading for the door, his garbage dropped in to the trash receptacle. Stephen followed, his steps slow as fatigue hit.

Kitlin turned from the window in Kieren's room, studying the room and then her parents. There had been no question that they were all kept together. She was just tired of ending up in a hospital room. Kieren had not roused and that was concerning. No one knew exactly what had happened to him.

She found that she just couldn't pray. Not at that point. Her words didn't seem to reach past the ceiling. Frustrated, she walked to the door and pulled it open and walked through. Her parents watched her before sharing a look. They were frustrated and worried as well.

Frankie watched as Kitlin walked towards him. She's angry, he thought. She's angry and ready to go on the offensive. And we can't have her doing that.

"Frankie? What did you find?"

"Not a lot. The assailants didn't go in much past the doorway, given that they closed the door behind them. Your apartment has not been disturbed, if that's what you are asking."

"That's not what I'm asking. I am asking how close you are to solving this."

"We're getting close, Kitlin." Frankie became stern with her. "We need to work through what we have. What we have been given. And we have other cases that we're working on." Frankie's words had a bite to them.

"We know that, Frankie. We get that. But this has gone too far." Kitlin walked away, towards Streeter who stood waiting for her, Richard and Timothy at his side.

Chapter 41

Streeter sat back, his mind racing at what Kitlin had asked. He had not expected it from her. He searched her face and then the faces of her parents. Richard had not said much, but he knew what she was wanting to do.

"Will this work? Streeter, can we do this without putting anyone at the station in danger?" Kitlin searched their faces, seeing Abe and Murphy sitting nearby. They had appeared at some point over the evening. Doug was with them, an interested look on his face. Darcy had warned them that Kitlin would go on the offensive with Kieren being hurt.

"It will. We can prepare the ads, start running them, and go from there. I have already spoken with our lawyer and he is on board with this." Streeter looked around. "I know Frankie will be vocal about this."

"He always is. He has to be, given that he's an officer." Doug finally spoke, bringing their attention to him. "But I agree. Going on the offensive is how you have to work it. Can we help plan the ads?"

"You can." Kitlin pulled out a folded piece of paper. "This is what we were thinking. Take a look at it, change it as you think it needs to be changed. I'm fine with that." She was on her feet, heading for Kieren's room, seeing her father standing waiting for her. She walked into his hug, hearing his prayer for her and Avery.

"Dad?"

"It's a step that we've prayed about. We'll get through this and get your fellow back to you."

"I just pray that it works. Avery needs to come home. His family needs him." Kitlin moved past him towards Kieren, finding him starting to rouse. Her mother simply wrapped her in a hug.

Doug studied the paper before he passed it to Abe, who read it, his eyes raising to watch Paul. He nodded.

"She's good. She says what she wants to, challenges them, but doesn't give anything away." Abe looked towards Streeter. "When do you plan on starting these?"

"Tomorrow, during Avery's normal hours. Craig has agreed to that, in fact, is eager to do this."

"That makes sense. Just give Frankie or Caleb a head's up on that." Murphy rose, heading for the hallway, walking through it just to see if anyone was there that shouldn't be. It was after visiting hours. None of them should be there but Caleb had cleared it for them to be there. It was one way to keep the family all together.

Frankie stood the next morning in the reception area at the radio station, listening to the ad that was running. He was disturbed, to say the least. He had not expected Kitlin to take this step. Caleb had shaken his head and grinned for a moment, simply stating that he really didn't know Kitlin if he thought she would not do what she had threatened to do.

"I agree with what she has done, Frankie." Streeter stood almost toe to toe with Frankie. "This case is not moving anywhere. You have had no other contact with Avery or his abductors. For all we know, he could be dead and his body gotten rid of."

Frankie stared around the reception area, looking for answers and not finding any. He shivered for a moment, knowing that Streeter was correct.

"If you can any response, I want to know." Frankie walked away, leaving Streeter staring after him.

Kitlin disappeared into his office where she took refuge when Frankie had appeared. She did not want to face him. Richard had simply grinned, closed the door, and stood against it. He searched the office, taking in the photos on the walls, the awards, the license, and then dropped to the desk top. Kitlin paced in what area that she could.

"You're not sure that you made the right decision, are you?" Richard grinned at her again, seeing her discomfort.

"No, I'm not. But we needed to do something. This is the only thing that I could do. You won't let me walk down the street on my own." She smirked at his laugh.

"No, we won't do that. I don't want to have to answer to Avery if you're hurt. And how is Kieren today?"

"Not well. He took a hard beating, as Dad says. He'll be in the hospital for a few days. Then Abe is moving us all out to his compound."

"He will do that. It's likely the best place for you all. Just don't talk with Ian. He'll want to fly you away somewhere to hide." Richard began to laugh at the expression of shock on her face.

"He will do what?" Her voice rose in surprise before she clapped her hands across her mouth.

"That's what he does. He offers to fly the ladies in danger somewhere safe."

"I pity his young daughter. She'll never have a boyfriend." She smirked once more as Richard continued to laugh, moving away from the door as Streeter knocked at it.

"Sounds as if Richard has everything under control in here." Streeter began to laugh as well, being good friends with Richard. They had shared many a cup of coffee, a meal, and Bible study, and prayer. "Frankie was not happy, but we knew that already."

"I don't care. If it works, it's worth it. Where am I to go tonight, Richard?"

"Back to the hospital. I heard that Kieren will be released tomorrow. Matt is a paramedic, so it works to have you at Abe's. We also have a friend who is an emergency physician and he will be around as will his wife who is a nurse."

"God at work again, is what you're telling me?" Kitlin grew sober. "Where is he, Richard? When will Avery be home?"

———

Chapter 42

The man holding Avery spun as he heard the radio station playing Kitlin's ad. His face grew black as anger raged within him. He stared at the walls around him, not seeing the expensive wall treatment, the expensive art work, the expensive furniture, or the expensive floor covering. He only saw that Avery was a problem, a problem that he had to deal with but he could not get rid of him. Not yet, he decided. He still had use for him.

Theo watched from outside the room. He knew better than to approach his employer when he was in a mood like that. He had set the sting his rage could project. And he had no wish to feel that again. Saul was still in jail, awaiting trial on some of the charges he faced. His courier work had gone to someone else.

His employer reached for his phone, barking out orders to whoever it was. His lawyer merely remained silent, knowing from experience that he could not get a word in. He simply hung up the phone and stared at it. He had had enough. Turning to his filing cabinets, he sorted through files and pulled the ones that he wanted. Walking from his building, he headed for the police station, ready to talk to someone.

Frankie looked up as the desk officer appeared in his doorway, his thought on another investigation that he was deep into.

"Jason?"

———

"James Walton is here. He wants to speak with you. He says it's about this case with Avery and Kitlin."

"He does?" Frankie stared at him for a moment before he was on his feet. "Put him in one of the interrogation rooms. I need to speak with Caleb." He was away, searching for Caleb. "Caleb? James Walton is here, something about Avery and Kitlin."

Caleb looked up from the budget allocations that he had been contemplating, trying to make them work.

"James Walton? The man's lawyer? That is interesting. Go and see what he has to say. Then come and find me." Caleb squinted at the clock and sighed. He had planned to be away on time tonight, but that didn't seem to be happening.

"No, go home, Caleb. Spend time with your family. Your three kids need your attention. I'll catch up with you later by phone or in the morning."

Frankie listened to what James Walton had to say, taking his notes. He knew that he would need to verify everything but that would not be a problem. He looked with interest at the file folders sliding across the table towards him.

"Why, James? Why come in now?"

"Because he needs to be stopped. He won't stop on his own. He is out of control." James looked repentant. "I had no idea that he had kidnapped the two. If I had, I would have been here sooner. I'm sorry. I wish I knew where he has hidden Avery. I would tell you." James paused, trying to control his emotions. "I never knew that he was so deep in crime. I mean, I heard the rumours but if I approached him, he always denied it."

"I understand, James. You're free to go. Just be very careful. In fact, I would suggest that you leave town tonight and have no contact with anyone here. Here's my card. Call me with anything else."

Frankie watched him walk away before he turned back to his office. This had made a lot more work for him, work that he had to set aside for the moment. He looked at the clock, and then grabbed his jacket. He needed to head home. Tomorrow was a new day and he would start fresh.

Kitlin found herself pacing the cabin that her family was now housed in. She knew that Richard was around and would be until the next day. At that point, a new team led by a man named Don would take over. And Abe's men were starting to make her feel smothered. Kieren was home and now asleep, his body trying to recover from his beating. He could give no further information. In fact, he didn't remember the beating at all.

The next day, Kitlin listened to the ads running once more. Streeter had agreed to run them three times a day for five days. Then, they would reassess the success of them. Kitlin had not been in agreement with that but she could understand his reasoning.

Frankie had stood in the doorway of the cabin around noon, his eyes on Kitlin before moving to Kieren. Their parents were away, heading back to their hometown to sign paperwork on their house. He had made sure that officers had gone with them, not taking a chance on having them disappear.

"Frankie? What are you saying?" Kitlin was quite sure that she had heard him rightly. She stood at the window, the sun beating down on the snow and melting it, almost too bright to look at.

"That your ads have worked. Almost too well. We had a lawyer come in last night with information for us. And no, I am not telling you who. But he did work for the man we suspect."

"A criminal himself?" Kieren watched his sister closely, seeing how tense she was.

"No, not at all. He was not involved in any crimes. He likely has another lawyer for that. He has given us a lot of information that we need to investigate and verify. Jake and I have been pulled back to work on that. We'll find Avery. And soon."

"I pray that you do. I worry that he won't come home unless you do."

Kieren moved to hug his sister, feeling her tears against his shoulder. He looked around at Frankie, who simply nodded and walked away. This needed to end. Only none of them knew just how to do that.

God, this would be a good time for a miracle. We need to find him, but I am not sure that he will be alive when we do. Protect him, please dear Lord.

Chapter 43

The day that Avery disappeared, he had simply walked to the vehicle and climbed in, knowing that he had no choice. He wouldn't make it back into the building in time, not with the man standing behind him. He had flinched when his hands were bound and then a blindfold and gag slapped around his face. He listened closely, but the men weren't speaking. And he couldn't tell what direction they were heading.

Pulled from the vehicle, Avery was shoved forward, a hand on his arm the only thing keeping him upright. He stumbled up the stairs, through a hallway, and then down some more stairs. He tripped and fell to his knees, the shock of landing on rock reverberating through his body. Hauled to his feet, he was shoved forward, landing once more on rock. The door slammed behind him, leaving a cruel, vicious laugh echoing around him.

He stayed that way for a moment, before he turned to sit, reaching to pull off the gag and blindfold. He stared at his wrists and then began to bite at the knot, finally managing to free himself.

Rising to his feet, Avery explored the room, noting the small window at one end but the rough stone walls and floor. There was no way that he could make it out. Not on his own. And his phone? It not likely would be able to send out any signal from within the room.

Sighing to himself, Avery lowered himself back to the floor, finding a corner away from the door. He stretched out his legs, crossing his ankles, his hands jammed into his jacket pockets. The room was not cold but slightly chilly. I'm underground again, he decided. And now, Lord, a captive again.

Time passed before he dozed off. He didn't hear the door squeak open, jumping slightly in his sleep. Theo stood there, gloating that they had Avery back in their custody. He would not escape this time. He still could not understand how he had escaped the last time. There just wasn't an explanation for that.

The next morning, Avery roused, the small shaft of sun shining down on him. He stood, looking around, disoriented for a moment. He walked to the small bathroom, running the water as hot as he could, washing at his face. He removed his jacket, dropping it back into the corner that he had chosen would be where he made his stand.

Theo stood in the doorway an hour later, watching Avery. They were in a standoff, Avery not moving forward as commanded, Theo not moving into the room. How long they would have stood there, they were ever sure afterwards. There were footsteps behind Theo before he stepped backwards, slamming the door behind him. The lock clicked into place.

Avery drew a deep breath, thankful for the moment that he had escaped whatever it was that he faced. His prayer was that Kitlin was safe, that they had not been able to reach through to her. He prayed as he had never prayed before, drawing on his long line of memorization to find the verses that would calm him. And calm him they did. Avery decided that he was no longer a pauper, that what he had been going through was no longer draining his heart and soul. God had brought him home once more and he was thankful for that.

A day passed that way, Theo appearing every couple of hours in the doorway. He didn't say anything, just stood and stared at Avery. Avery just stared back. He waited for food to be brought to him, but that didn't happen. He was able to find water to drink, but he knew that he needed food.

The next day, things changed. Theo appeared, this time with another man, heavyset like himself. This man walked into the room, grasping Avery's arm tightly, and then pulling him from the room. Taken to the room in the basement that had seen rough use, Avery paled, knowing that he might not make it out of that room. He could feel the evil there.

Hearing footsteps behind, Avery froze, his breath catching in his chest. This is it, he thought. This is where whatever it is happens. He didn't hear anything more but was afraid to move.

The man stood and watched Avery, gloating that he was back in their control. This is where he would end it all. Avery would serve his purpose and then die. That he had determined would happen. And no one would stand in the way. Not any more. He still didn't understand how the two had managed to escape from him before.

Forced to stand there for hours, Avery grew weary. He was not allowed to slump, a blow to his

———

210

back making him stand upright once more. Returned to the room, Avery dropped to the floor, his head burrowing against his upraised knees. His despair was growing minute by minute. He turned at long last, crawling across the floor to find his jacket, pulling it on, and then shifting to lean into the corner. His eyes closed and he slept.

The next day, he was roused from his sleep and forced once more from the room. Avery was growing desperate, anxious to get away, but not knowing how to do that. The man stood behind him, this time with a paper in his hand.

"Avery Dennis. You will help me." His rough coarse voice grated against Avery. "You will help me with what I am planning." He drew closer, finally coming to stand in front of Avery, papers held out in front of him. "You will sign these papers, admitting your guilt to many crimes."

Avery shook his head, his eyes not wavering from the man.

"That won't happen." His simple statement enraged the man. "I have committed no crimes. People will know that that that statement would be false."

Avery's words and his denial to help enraged the man even further. No matter how much Avery was threatened or his family threatened, he simply stood silent, refusing to take the papers or the pen held in front of him.

The man looked around, anger driving what he needed to be done. He finally motioned to the man as he walked away. They stood for a moment in conference, before the older man left. Theo stood and studied Avery, admiration in his glance for a man who stood true to his convictions. Only that stance would not help him at this point. Drawing on gloves, the man approached Avery.

"All you have to do is sign these papers." Theo once more stated the obvious.

Avery shook his head, not budging.

"No, I won't. I can't lie to save him. And that is what he wants. His whole life is built on a lie."

Chapter 44

Theo realized at that point that Avery would not give in. He had hoped that he would. He studied his gloved hands and then Avery. A fist drawn back was then driven into Avery's abdomen, doubling him over and causing him to wrap his arms around himself. Theo's fists continued to pummel Avery, until he stopped. His breath came roughly for a moment. Shaking his head, Theo drew off his gloves and walked away. The other man dragged Avery back to his dungeon and dropped him there. Avery didn't move from where he was dropped. The beating had been brutal, driving him down into depths within himself that he didn't know existed.

Theo returned an hour later, rolling Avery over to his back. A camera flashed before he studied the photo and nodded. It was graphic enough, he thought. This should work to bring Kitlin out to where they could capture her again. Having her here and threatened would surely make Avery sign what he had been asked to.

That photo was the one that Kitlin received. Theo had used a throwaway phone and then done just that with the phone. It had been smashed to pieces and the pieces thrown into the garbage.

Avery lay there for days, briefly rousing to alertness, but never enough to fully understand what

was being yelled at him. He just didn't care anymore.
The darkness that he was in just didn't release him.

Then one day, the room was unlocked, and a man
stood there. He looked around but didn't see the men
who should have been there. He reached to draw
Avery to his feet, draping him over a shoulder, and
then walked away with him, to the outdoors. He laid
Avery down before he drew out a phone. Studying it,
he knew that he had to call for help.

"Brennan." Frankie's voice barked out his name.
He was deep into research on a case, having set aside
Avery's case. He was waiting on information and just
couldn't find the one part that he needed.

"Frankie? It's Jimmy. I have Avery."

"Jimmy? You have Avery?" Frankie was on his
feet, reaching for his jacket and his keys. "Where?"

"At the old Walton place. He's been using it for
keeping Avery here. He was in the rock basement, in
the old root cellar."

"Okay. I'm on my way."

"Wait, Frankie. Come on your own and come in
from the side road. Not the driveway. I've headed that
way and will meet you there."

Frankie paused for a moment before he nodded.
He hesitated to ask but knew that he had to.

"Jimmy? Is he alive?"

"He is, but he's hurt very badly. He'll need to be
hospitalized. They beat him well. And I have the
information that they wanted him to sign."

———

"You do? I'm not asking how you did that. I'll find you and then work on warrants to go in."

"That's what you need to do."

Jimmy watched Avery closely, concerned about him. He ducked down further as he heard a vehicle before he was on his feet, Avery in his arms, heading for Frankie's car. He stuffed Avery into the passenger's seat, handed over the paperwork, and then disappeared. Frankie had looked down for a moment to assess Avery. When he looked up, Jimmy was gone. Where did he go, Frankie asked himself? He does this all the time.

Pulling up to the ambulance bay, Frankie was out of the car, running inside for help. Parking his vehicle out of the way, he ran back inside, watching as the physician began his assessment of Avery.

"Doc? What can you tell me?" Frankie moved closer.

"He's been beaten and badly. A least a couple of days. Where was he?"

"That's part of the investigation that I can't go into. Listen. I'm pulling in officers to be with him. They stay with him no matter where he goes. This is attempted murder."

"I understand. There is no problem. Call me in an hour and I'll have a better report for you. His family?" He looked around at that, not hearing Frankie speak.

"I'll bring them in. There is also a lady who needs to be here."

"Do what you need to. I'll authorize them all to see him. Now, away with you."

Frankie walked rapidly through the department building, looking for Caleb. He finally tracked him down in a conference room, seated at a table, reading through reports. He sat, his jacket off, trying to catch his breath.

Caleb eyed him, not quite sure what Frankie was up to or where he had been.

"Frankie? Care to explain?"

"I will." Frankie shook his head, not quite believing what he had just seen. "We have Avery. Jimmy came through."

"Jimmy? When?" Caleb laid down his paperwork, shifting in his chair to face Frankie. He didn't hear the murmurs around him, the click of the computer keyboards, or the ringing of the odd phone.

"Just now. I went out and found them. Avery is in the hospital. He has been beaten badly and is unconscious. I have the address. We can work on warrants now and go in and search the place. Jimmy also gave me some paperwork that he says Avery was being forced to sign. Only Avery refused. That likely led to his beating."

"That I would agree with." Caleb rose. "I'll go find Michael and Meg. And then Aubrey and Aveleen. Hannah will be relieved as well."

"Hannah needs to be with her aunt and uncle. Peg will take your kids. I called her and asked her if she would, without saying much other than that

Hannah was needed to be with her family. I hope and pray that I didn't leave the wrong impression with her."

"I'm sure that Peg will be fine. I'll call Hannah and Hannah can put her mind at ease."

Chapter 45

Michael and Meg sat, arms around one another. This was not the first time that they had sat like this, feeling alone, waiting for word on one of their children. Their only consolation was that Avery was the last one of them. They prayed that no other family member faced what they had. Caleb had just appeared at their door earlier, stepping inside. He had scared Meg with the grim look on his face before it softened and he had smiled as he hugged the woman who he called aunt.

"We have Avery, Michael. Meg. He's alive."

His words had stopped them for a moment before Michael reached to rest his hands on Caleb's shoulders. He couldn't quite believe the words being spoken.

"I'm sorry. You said that you have Avery?"

"We do. Someone found him, called Frankie, and Frankie brought him to the hospital. That's where I'm heading with you two." He watched with compassion as Meg began to weep, Michael's arms around his wife before they separated, to find their coats and Meg her purse.

"How is he, Caleb? Do you know?" Meg's voice was broken but joyful at the same time.

"He's unconscious. As you know, he was beaten. The physician was assessing him when

Frankie came back. We can now end this for you." Caleb paused as Michael's phone rang.

"Dad? Any word?" Aubrey's voice echoed over the line. He had given up all hope that he would see his younger brother again.

"Head for the hospital, son. Is Aveleen with you?"

"She is, Dad. But why? The hospital? I don't understand."

"We have Avery, Aubrey. Frankie found him. He's at the hospital. Caleb is here to take your mother and me there. We will meet you all there." Michael closed and locked the door behind him, his eyes sliding closed as he fought the tears trickling down his face. Thank you, Lord, was his whisper as he stared up at the clear blue sky. A solitary cloud drifted by. The day was warmer and the snow had melted. He was just thankful.

"Caleb? Kitlin?" Meg's soft question caught at Caleb's ear as he paused at a red light. "We need her here."

"I know. I called Abe. He'll get her and her family in. Kieren is on his feet and should be reassessed as well. We can have that done at the same time we're waiting for word on Avery." He paused once more in his words. He just didn't know what to say. God had been there all along, he acknowledged, even when they had doubted that Avery would be found and found alive.

———

Kitlin paced the cabin, feeling housebound and broken. She just wanted to see Avery, to know that he was alive. But that hadn't been forthcoming. She was desperate to escape. Streeter had called her earlier, just to check in on her. He had been optimistic that their scheme was working. Only she no longer believed that it was.

Kieren watched his sister closely, seeing something different about her that day. He frowned, before he shared a look with his parents. They both nodded before Paul headed for the door. He stood back to let Abe enter, seeing the other seven men standing outside as well as Richard's full team. Something was up, he thought.

"Abe?" Kitlin's voice was barely audible as she paled. Abe had that look about him that spelled bad news, she thought.

"Kitlin? We've come to take you all to town." Abe's gentle smile broke through the stern look on his face.

"To town?" Kitlin approached him. "I don't understand." When Abe just continued to smile, Kitlin's smile broke out, lighting up her face. "What time?"

"Time? About an hour ago." Abe reached to hug her, then turned to the others. "We have Avery. Frankie found him and brought him to safety. Don't ask how as that is part of the investigation."

"I don't care how. As long as he's alive and with us, that's all that matters."

The four watched as Kitlin almost danced to her bedroom, returning with her coat. She glared at them.

"Well? What are we standing around here for? Aren't we heading for town?" She was through the door, hugging each one of the team members waiting for her before she ran for Abe's SUV.

"I guess that we were told." Kieren rose carefully to his feet, taking with thanks the jacket handed him. "Kitlin has spoken. Let's go."

Kitlin hesitated as she walked through the doors, searching for someone. Only she didn't know who. Her eyes were drawn to the man, dressed in black, who stood against a wall. She approached him, not seeing Murphy and Nathaniel trailing after her.

"Thank you. I don't know your name, but you saved us once. And now saved Avery." She reached to hug him before she stood back. "I don't need to know your name. I just know that God sent you to help us. You may be a man, but you are our angel." She turned, momentarily blinded by her tears before she felt a hand leading her away.

Jimmy nodded, watching her walk away from him before he looked up. A smile crossed his face and then he too walked away. Nathaniel was watching him. He blinked and when he looked again, Jimmy was gone. He spun, trying to find him and not able to. Shaking his head, he pondered Kitlin's words. Maybe, he thought, just maybe she was right. He was an angel sent from God just for this.

Abe watched the families closely, standing next to Richard. Their work was almost finished once

---

again. And once again, their friends were safe. He knew that there was still work to do but that would come. He studied the waiting room, taking in the soft cream walls, the colourful chairs, the tables with their magazines and toys for kids, and the gray tiled floor.

"How many times have we stood here, Richard?"

"Far too many. Far too many of our friends, including you and Emma, have been here in very stages of injury and almost death. I pray that this is the last of our friends to face this." Richard walked away, Abe's soft "me, too" echoing in his ears.

Chapter 46

Two days later, Avery shifted on the bed. He was hurting in more ways than one, he thought. But he was free. He knew from Frankie that arrests were imminent and that he would still be under guard for the next day or so. That didn't matter. Not any more.

He watched as Kitlin wandered his hospital room. She had not said much as yet, but he knew that she had been very worried. Kieren had made a point of telling him that. His father and hers had told him of her plans with the ads and that they had actually gone ahead with that. He had asked if she had been hurt at all. When they said no, he sighed and then simply stated it was okay. He understood.

His hand out, Avery waited for Kitlin to take his. He smiled as she studied it and then him before hers reached for his. He tugged her closer, wrapping her in his arms, not letting her see the pain that action caused.

"I'm so glad that you're here, Kitlin. I dreamed about you when we were apart. I was so afraid that he would get you." His words were muffled against her hair.

"I know. I was so afraid as well that he would kill you. That was his plan, I think."

"It was, sweetheart, but we didn't let him win. God didn't let him win. Although I can't figure out how I got away." He felt her shifting in his arms and drew her down beside him. "What is it?"

"It was our angel, Avery. He found you. Frankie said his name is Jimmy, and he thinks that he is a flesh-and-blood man. Nathaniel talked to me when we were waiting for word that night. He said he blinked and Jimmy disappeared. I still say that he was our angel."

"That he could be. Now, when can I leave?"

"Tomorrow. Your mom wants you to go to their place for a couple of days."

"Only if you do too. We've been apart for too long, through too much. I want to start dating you, if you will allow me to."

Kitlin turned her face to his, a thoughtful look on her face.

"We can do that. Thank you, Avery. You have drawn me back from where I was. I felt like a pauper, that God had walked away and left me without anything."

"I felt the same for months. I know that He didn't but that's how we feel at times." He looked around as the door opened and Frankie appeared. "And here's Frankie and Caleb. What brings you two here?"

"Good news, you two. We have made all the arrests that we need to. Holding you in that building, Avery? That sealed his fate as we say."

"It did?" Kitlin frowned at them. "Okay, start talking. I want all the nitty-gritty details."

The men laughed at her before Frankie handed over a photo.

"This is the man who was behind it all, Kitlin. A well-known businessman here in town, although not one who's well-loved."

"I would gather that he wouldn't be. Why?"

"Greed. Plain and simple greed." Caleb spoke up at that point. "It does go back to when you were young, Avery, just about two years old. He had returned here from another town and thought that he should be prominent in town right away. When he wasn't, he looked around for someone to blame. For reasons he is refusing to say, he fixated on your father. That drove him to crime, again why he won't say. He was determined to be the richest man in town, thinking that riches would buy him good will and happiness. Only, it didn't. The men and women under him are talking. He's got a lot to answer for just here in town, but his reach stretched to other towns."

"Andrew and Bill?" Avery's voice echoed Frankie's unspoken thoughts.

"Exactly." Frankie retrieved the photo. "We understand that when you were taken from the radio station, Kitlin was incidental to it. They saw you two talking, thought that you were closer than you were, and took her to put pressure on you. It backfired on them in a way."

"His son committed suicide about a year ago. He just couldn't take what he found his father to be. There was just too much shame. We do know from paperwork that we found when we searched his home that he planned to have you sign paperwork, Avery, to admit that you were into crime. And then the plan was

---

to kill you, staging it as a suicide with a suicide note from you.”

Kitlin paled as she shrank back against Avery, who tightened his hug.

“He’s brutal, to say the least, isn’t he?” Avery finally spoke, his thoughts troubled. To think that he would go to all that work for what?”

“That’s it, Avery.” Caleb and Frankie shared looks. There was information that would come out at trial but for now would stay within the investigation. “Saul and Theo are finally talking as our those under him. His wife? She committed suicide about three years ago. The word we’re receiving is that her son was never the same after that.”

“That’s so sad.” Kitlin blinked as the men grew silent, each lost in their own thoughts.

Frankie studied the couple in front of him. Thank You, Lord, for Your protection for these two. They have been through so much, granted not as much as others.

“Theo is searching, Avery. He has asked to speak with Greg. Your witness reached through to him. He wanted to know if you would ever consider visiting him.”

Avery nodded, knowing that at some point, he would.

“Not at the moment. We need to get through the trials, just so nothing can be said that I tampered with anything.” Avery began to pray once more for his captors. Maybe this was why he went through what he did.

"Frankie, what about Jimmy?" Kitlin's question broke into the stillness that had lasted for a few moments.

"Jimmy? What about him?" Caleb shared a look with Frankie.

"I wish I could speak with him again, just to thank him." Kitlin saw the look that the two officers shared.

"The thing of it is, Kitlin, is that Jimmy can't be found. It's almost as if he was never here."

Kitlin gave a soft smile, feeling Avery's arm tighten around her.

"An angel sent by God, to protect and save us." She stared past the men, seeing Jimmy standing there for a moment before he touched his forehead and disappeared from sight. Avery's arm tightened more around her, and she knew that he had seen Jimmy as well.

The two officers didn't know what to say at that. That had been their thought, only they had never expressed it to one another.

Six months later, Avery paced the office of their minister, Greg Evans. He stared down at his suit, not used to wearing one before he reached to touch the yellow rose on his lapel. His beloved Kitlin had agreed to marry him after he had courted her for months. She had stood in front of him as he went down on one knee, reaching for her hand, a beautiful rose-gold ring with a ruby stone in his hands. Tears had sparked on both their faces when she had simply nodded. He had risen to his feet, gathered her close, and kissed her.

Aubrey watched his brother, knowing somewhat how he felt. He knew that Avery would have prayed over this step before he made it. That was who his brother was. His adventure had deepened his faith. Everyone around him could see that.

Michael stood in the doorway, his eyes on his sons. *One is already married, with a little one on the way, and the other son is now taking that step. We prayed for their life mates all these years, and You have provided the ones that they need. Not the ones that we may have chosen for them. In Your wisdom, Lord, You have brought them through a fire and out the other side, scarred, yes, but complete in You.*

"Son, let me pray with you once more before we head out to meet your bride. I hear that she is very beautiful and that you won't be able to speak when you see her." Michael wrapped his son into a hug, feeling the little boy in Avery's grasp but also the man who stood before him.

Later that afternoon, Avery stood, his arms around his beloved Kitlin, thinking how beautiful she was in her simple, lace-covered white dress, his yellow roses somewhere on a table. She leaned back against him, not quite sure that the day was real. Their friends and family were mingling around them, making use of the large yard behind the home that her parents had purchased in Riverville.

"Do you know how much I love you?" Avery's voice was whispered in her ear.

"I do know, but I don't want you to ever stop telling me that. I love you so much." Kitlin leaned harder on him. "Avery, would we have met?"

"Would we have met? You mean if we hadn't gone through what we did?"

Kitlin nodded, not quite sure how to express her thoughts.

"That's what I mean. I know that I had taken work at the station, but I wasn't really planning on moving here. I just knew that I wanted to go somewhere I could try and stand on my own two feet. I mean, Mom and Dad let me. Kieren was learning to stand back and let me make my own decisions and mistakes."

"We would have, sweetheart. I truly believe that God had determined before time began that you and I would meet and join our lives." He rested his chin on her head, thoughts going through his mind at what they had faced. "I am just so thankful that He led us through to the other side. Dad said that we have scars, and he is correct in that."

"War wounds, my love. War wounds." Kitlin grew thoughtful, her eyes on Frankie and Caleb before they sought out each of Abe's team members and then Richard's team. "We have so many friends."

"We do. And they can understand to a certain extent what we have gone through. That helps to heal us, to be able to talk with them."

"It does." Kitlin shifted on her feet, not used to wearing dress shoes. "Have you thought any more about what Streeter asked you?"

"About taking over the station? We have been praying about that, sweetheart, and I think we are agreed on that. Your father has approached Streeter, wanting to invest in a company here in town. Streeter told me earlier today that they had come to an agreement on that. Your dad will become a partner, with him. Streeter will stay on for now, training someone to take over for him."

"But it's not you. You enjoy your show too much. Your golden-oldies. And if you gave that up, how could you use your sign off?" She laughed at him. "You won't be able to say "see you on the flipside" if you were not there. You are where God has placed you."

"And you? You're content not going back?" Avery knew her answer but just had to ask.

———

230

"I am. I never really fit in there. I'll find something to do. Kieren has asked me to manage his office for now. I would like that. He's getting busier than he thought he would ever be."

"That's what Timothy has said. He's finding people to help him. And those people are ones who are down on their luck, needing a hand up."

"That's what Kieren has said. That's what he has always wanted to do, to be a blessing that way." Kitlin turned in his arms, her arms around him.

"That is it." Avery studied her before he bent to kiss her. "I love you, sweetheart. Don't ever change."

———

231

Thank you for choosing the story of Avery and his Kitlin, the last of the three Dennis siblings. Once more, the characters have chosen their story, adding to it as they see fit. As an author, I am only along for the ride and to put into words their story.

What are you struggling with today? Do you feel like Avery and Kitlin, a pauper in your walk with God? My father often said that like the Israelites, we can wander into the desert and need to be brought back. That drought is where we find ourselves as pauper. God never moves. He never leaves or forsakes us. No matter what we face, He is there, in the midst, sheltering us, drawing us closer, using us as a blessing for many.

Now, once more, these unruly characters have drawn in many characters. Abe and his team's stories are in *His Guardians*. Doug and Darcy are in *The Heart of a Lion*. Dave and Rylee's is in *A Touch of His Garment*. Andrew and Phoebe's is *The Potter's Hands*. Bill and Cora's is *Hidden in the Hollow*. Samuel and Aideen's are part of *His Warriors* series. I think that covers them all. Aubrey and Finlee's is *The Prodigal*. Aveleen and Logan's is *The Princess*, part of *Children of His Promise* series. All these can be found on my website. ronnabacon.com.

This brings to the close of another series, *His Searchers*. I have no idea what lies next, although the idea of a series based on the five wise virgins is percolating in my brain and one of the stories has been started. I will see where I go from there. And Richard and his team and Don and his team are throwing hints that maybe their stories should be told.

God bless each one of you. May you continue to find His blessing on your life as you walk through each day.

Ronna